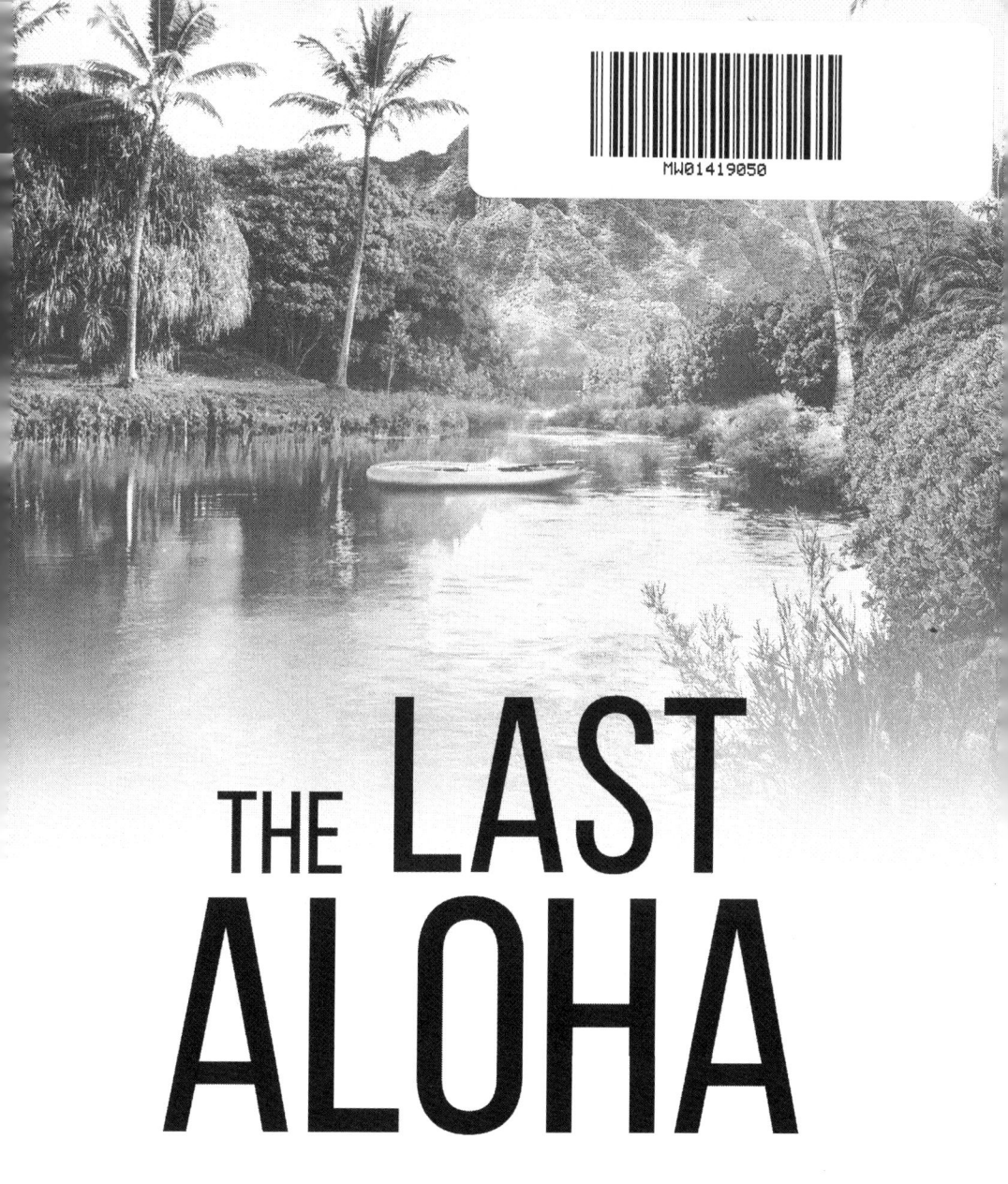

# THE LAST ALOHA

A.J. RIVERS
& THOMAS YORK

***The Last Aloha***

# PROLOGUE

***Hilton Garden Inn***
***Honeymoon Suite***
***Island of Kauai***
***October 7th, 2023***
***Midnight***

Alton Lincoln watched the silver crest of a moonlit wave crash against the rocky coast of Kauai. While rubbing his wrists, he was enraptured with the ebb and flow of the timeless drift of the ocean. His ears perked up to the call of nightbirds and the hum and drum of mountain crickets farther up in the jungle canopy. As he took in a slow, peaceful breath in this natural paradise, he heard the thunderous roar of a distant storm and savored the powerful fragrance of plumeria emanating from the jungle surrounding his honeymoon bungalow.

After a few moments, he rubbed his wrists again, pushing back the occasional numbness he felt sometimes when the weather was about to change. Alton turned from the beautiful, crystalline waters and paused for a moment to glance at the long shadows of the jungle. Taking in one last view of the mysterious primeval place, brooding with darkness and mystery, he walked back inside. Now, his eyes stayed fixed lovingly on the sleeping blonde-haired vision of beauty that was his sleeping bride—Candace Kincaid.

*Candace Kincaid Lincoln,* he reminded himself. He took a deep sigh and smiled warmly as she purred like a kitten in her sleep. He was truly having the time of his life on his new adventure with his new wife. How her face seemed to radiate warmth and love even as she dreamed.

It was even more beautiful than she had looked on their wedding day, just a few days ago, but so firm, so solid, that it felt like it was a lifetime ago. Like it had always been there, had always been meant to be, and now their honeymoon stretched on into an eternity of bliss. Memories danced in his vision just like the dappled moonlight on the water. Her gorgeous white lace dress and the bright Hawaiian *lei* that she'd worn. Her smile, brighter than the sun.

*The plumeria flowers had fallen all around us just as Wayne Toups started wailing away "New Orleans Ladies." We moved in time, and I felt the softness of her body swaying with mine. How Candace's blue eyes sparkled in the glow of the torch lights as she kissed me.*

Overwhelmed in the moment, he wiped away a happy tear. How had he ended up in such bliss? Was he worthy of such happiness in his life after all he had suffered? Somehow, he couldn't shake that feeling that always seemed to stay even in the happiest of moments—uncertainty. It was that soul-crushing unease that, at any moment, his legs could be cut out from under him, and all of his happiness and success could once again come crashing down.

As it once had years ago. That had been the humiliating and horrific Joanie Petre, his ex-wife. It had been toxic from the beginning with her—constant fights, screaming arguments, and petty slights. The relationship had been terrible, the marriage worse, and somehow the divorce process was so hellish that Alton had seriously considered—a few times—just giving up and consigning himself to a life of misery. But Alton had endured far worse in his life than Joanie. Despite the pain and suffering in his life—a father who'd shot him in a crazed state, testifying against a baseball coach pedophile, and the grandfather who died in his arms from dementia, Alton swore to never be a victim. He always moved forward. But regret might linger for a moment.

He'd landed the biggest contract of his career back then with Yellowrock. Then on a flight to Malaysia, Joanie said they needed to talk.

# THE LAST ALOHA

It was just like her to spring that on him when he had no way of escaping. For eighteen interminable hours, cramped in tiny airplane seats, she'd laid out every grievance, dispute, complaint, outrage, simmering resentment, and passive-aggressive observation, culminating with the cherry on top that she'd been cheating on him. It was the worst experience of his life. And that was before the lawyers got involved.

But all of that melted away when he looked once again at his peacefully sleeping bride. She sighed softly, a perfect sound, and nestled into her pillow. The sight made him fall in love all over again.

He'd been pretty reluctant to jump back into a relationship for a long time after the way it all shook out with Joanie—but somehow, when he least expected it, a miracle happened. On a chilled, snowy night, he stumbled into the future love of his life. Alton shook his head at the memory.

It was Christmas time up in the Colorado mountains. Some much-needed time away after both his work. He'd been chopping wood for the fireplace in his rental cabin when she walked up and asked for help. Apparently that night, Candace had run out of gas on a back road near his cabin.

The storm had suddenly worsened, and with nowhere to go, Candace asked if she could stay. Not that she had much choice. Six inches of snow fell in the first hour. They'd only barely managed to get Candace's car in the parking spot behind the cabin before it was buried in a blanket of white.

It had been an instant attraction to say the least. Over the next few snow-filled days, the only thing hotter than the blaze in Alton's fireplace was the fire in Candace's eyes each time they kissed. As the wind howled, and the drifts of snow fell each of those wondrous Christmas nights, they kept each other safe and warm from the darkness. It was like something out of a romance novel.

*I thank God each day for Candace.*

Each time they looked at each other, he prayed Candace could read his thoughts.

*Candace, you were a Godsend up in the Tennessee mountains. I was bitter and angry about the whole mess with Joanie. It was a horrific and painful fall from grace for me. But I'd go through that hell all over again to find you.*

The happy memories were there again pushing back the shadows of darkness. In his mind he could see the plumeria flowers falling during his first married dance with Candace. He saw Candace's glowing smile from the Hawaiian torches flickering in the red and orange of fire light. Then he felt her swaying hips as good old Wayne Toups went to wailing away another Cajun ballad, "Take My Hand," as they danced through the night.

*I can't dwell on the mistakes of my past. I have to accept that pain and suffering are a part of life. They make you appreciate things more when everything is glowing and great. Especially now that I landed the Raylight contract for Yellowrock.*

He grabbed a bottle of chilled water from the fridge and chugged it down. Then he lovingly stared at his new bride with the kindest of eyes and the warmest of smiles.

*God! How Candace looks like a sleeping angel right now under the slight glow of the moonlight.*

He climbed back into bed, careful not to wake the love of his life, and fell back to sleep.

In the early hours before sunrise, Candace rolled over to him and embraced him firmly. He felt her kisses on his brow and her soft hands nestled firmly into his back pulling him nearer. He awoke and smiled at Candace devilishly and kissed her firmly on her rose red lips. That was all that was needed to kick off a roaring wave of carnal desire that engulfed both Alton and Candace as husband and wife. It was a searing bond and a precious memory that would last Alton all the days of his life.

Six hours later and one hot shower together, Mr. and Mrs. Alton Lincoln set out on their epic honeymoon adventure. They were kayaking down the wide expanse of Kauai's Waialua River. It was to be a jungle filled, joyous adventure that neither would ever forget.

Candace wiped a tear and smiled. Alton narrowed his stare, concerned. "Is everything okay, honey?"

"I'm just so happy being married to you." She moved in and kissed his cheek. Alton felt the sting of a bug. Most likely a mosquito. He waved it away but smiled at Candace.

"And here I was thinking you just put up with me for my money," he joked.

She pouted. "Alton…"

"I know, I know," he said, holding his hands out in defense. "I just couldn't resist."

She didn't like jokes about that. It was a discussion they'd had before. But he knew, deep down in his core, that it wasn't about his money at all. The passion and love and joy they shared couldn't be faked. Those first few days had been magical, and the months since had never slowed down. Indeed, he hadn't even revealed the true extent of the money he made until they'd already decided to move in together. Some of his associates harped on him about it, saying he was making the same mistake he'd made with Joanie, but he didn't believe them. And even if he did believe them, he didn't care.

Candace wasn't like that. She'd never hurt him that way.

"What do you think about a race?" she called over.

Alton looked over at Candace's bright grin as they entered their individual kayaks into the cool waters of the Waialua River. He chuckled and pointed at Candace's kayak already two lengths ahead of his. "It looks like someone has gotten two jumps ahead of me, Mrs. Lincoln."

Candace splashed back at Alton and giggled. "Touché, Mr. Lincoln. I'll slow down to let you catch up. You'd better not let me win, either."

Alton laughed then looked up to the beautiful blue sky. He took in the cool morning air and heard a distant group of kayakers coming up behind him. Then groaned as he heard the troublesome click of their cameras as they went past. He put his paddle in the water and thrust forward to catch up to Candace when he found himself suddenly breaking out into a cold sweat. He pushed his paddle, but it felt like it was moving through sludge, and he was getting short of breath.

"Come on, honey! You're lagging behind," Candace said. She turned back to him, but her face dropped immediately.

Alton couldn't even cry out for help. A fiery pain was surging through his hands and feet simultaneously. His eyes twisted and spasmed as well. Alton's pulse quickened, and he tried to scream for Candace's help, but the muscles in his jaw locked in place and his mouth was clamped shut like a steel trap. All his muscles were in vice-like, burning spasms including his heart. He tried earnestly to stop the seizing, but a third wave caused him to lose control of his bowels and his balance in the kayak. With a fourth knife-stabbing seizure—with his heart racing chaotically and his breathing labored from the loss of his diaphragmatic muscles—Alton felt the loss of all his muscles and plunged sideways into the dark depths of the river.

He tried to claw his way back up, but his hands were cramped. He tried to kick his legs to stay afloat, but they had locked up. Worst of all, he and Candace had shrugged off their cumbersome lifejackets earlier at Candace's request. Panicking and helpless beneath the silted waters, Alton, for the briefest moment felt hope when he saw Candace had paddled up to where he fell in.

*Candace will dive in and pull me to the shore. She'll do CPR or figure out what happened as we wait for 911 to arrive.*

*But why hasn't she dived in yet? And… Is she crying that I'm drowning?*

Candace felt relief as she paddled over to the spot where Alton had fallen in. It wasn't that everything had gone according to plan. Of course, there had been missteps setting him up. And for a brief moment she had felt something for the man drowning beneath her boat. Was it a need to save him? Could it have been remorse or pity? Was it regret? Or maybe, just maybe, she might have felt misgivings toward him in the end. But didn't she always have these intense, remorseful feelings when her targets had been eliminated?

*He wasn't a target. Alton was more.*

Naturally, these were just the same useless emotions that lately seemed to get in her way and stall her killings. Delays and missed deadlines which had angered her employer and might be her own undoing one day if she wasn't careful. Her boss didn't suffer lovesick fools.

But, yes, this target had been different. There was an appeal to the suffering he had endured. He'd literally climbed out of the pits of hell and been a better man for it. She would have liked to have had one more stroll on the beach with him. There was something endearing about his naivete and his boyish smile.

To her drowning husband, whose blue eyes went lifeless as he spasmed one last time, Candace maniacally moaned as tears fell from her eyes.

"Losing you is more than I can bear, dear... husband. All the pain, the suffering, and the betrayal on your journey are over."

Having spoken her last words to the man she'd kissed under the flowers, Candace reached down into a bag she had nestled in the kayak. Biting her lip as the tears fell like a Hawaiian rain, she opened the bag and pulled from it a handful of flame colored plumeria flowers. She put them to her nose and took in the fragrant scent of the plumeria. Then Candace Kincaid Lincoln tossed them over the very spot where her husband had drowned. She took the deepest of relieved sighs watching the orange, white, and yellow petals drift away along the river's swirling currents.

Then Candace heard the distant screams from a kayaking group behind her. Slowly she turned and looked at a short, stocky man who looked bewildered at her actions, putting on her finest crying face. Candace could care less for the outraged man's screams or the scowl he gave her as he prepared to dive in to 'save' Alton Lincoln.

Candace said as much without saying a word. Her annoyed gestures, her leering smile echoed her sentiments as he looked one more time at her then plunged beneath the silted depths of Waialua River.

# CHAPTER ONE

***FBI Field Office***
***Enterprise St***
***Kapolei, Hawaii***
***October 10, 2023***
***09:00 A.M.***

Agent Keith Benton sat outside SAC Charlton Harris's office, rubbing his chin and taking a sigh. The veteran FBI agent had the tired eyes and frame of a man who had endured almost four decades of catching criminals. Over the last few years though, he had known the time to turn in the badge was drawing close. Eight years ago, when his precious wife died of cancer, he'd almost carried through and done it. Now, here he was waiting patiently to finally do just that—retire. Or, if Harris worked his magic to motivate him to stay with the FBI, transfer to a cushy desk job somewhere on the mainland and dance his cares away.

There was a tap on the glass door by a chestnut-haired woman with a lithe frame—ASAC Rachel Gentry. She was getting his attention and ushering him to come on in. Keith stood and proceeded into Charlton's office.

*Well, folks, here goes nothing.*

Harris put his long right hand out in front of him and shook Keith's hand. Then he ushered him to sit before kicking things off. "Have a seat, Agent Benton. How can we help you today?"

Keith sat and furrowed his brow studying both Rachel and Charlton. He crossed his arms and leaned back. "Let's cut the small talk, boss. Both of you know I'm not a man to mince words. You know why I requested this meeting."

Rachel nodded to Charlton and shrugged. "We do, Keith. Are you sure you want to carry through this time? I know the last big case—The Jade Princess—racked all of our brains and wore all of us down. Now, more than ever, with the recent scandals and missteps in the FBI, we need your experience and expertise to—"

Keith grunted. "Save the pep talk for the rookies, Rachel. I've heard that same rhetoric since the damn eighties. Since before you were born."

Rachel chuckled a little self-effacingly. "You got me there."

"Look, I always said I'd know when to pull the plug. And to tell the truth, I'm kind of feeling like I've stayed a little past my welcome. We do good work here, and I know that, but this world is... well, frankly, it's a bit too much for an old man like me. I think the Jade Princess case was a fine last hurrah for me and the Bureau." He pushed his resignation letter and retirement paperwork in front of them. "Human Resources already started the process. Here's my resignation letter and retirement pack for you to sign."

Undaunted or persuaded by Keith's request, SAC Harris simply harrumphed. "Let's talk about this, Benton. You've never let a case get under your skin. Why the decision now after we closed that one in particular just last month?"

Keith looked out the window at the white rolling waves of Nimitz Beach. He wished in the moment he was sitting out in the surf with a Mai Tai—and happily retired. "I've never shown that the work bugged me is what you mean. But over forty years of the same crooks doing the same crimes, many of them getting off scot-free, I've seen enough. Please, just sign the packet and let me live out my last days in peace."

"Retirement is not you, Agent Benton, and you know it." Rachel sat beside him and patted him on the back. "Even when you're off duty, you're still on the job. Remember, we closed The Sneaky Tiki a few nights still ranting over unsolved cases from ten or twenty years ago. You'd come out of retirement after six months begging to get back to work out of boredom."

Keith sat up straight and cocked his head with a skeptical eye. "I promise you, Rachel, I won't get that bored. Especially after the last few years of rogue agents and FBI misfires in this office."

"All right. You seem to have made up your mind." Harris kept a tight, emotionless face. Keith, having known Charlton for years, knew this look was his poker face. He was going all in. Keith didn't like it.

Puzzled by Charlton bowing in so quickly, Keith went wide-eyed in disbelief. "Are you seriously going to accept my request to retire without a counteroffer or transfer possibility?"

Harris yawned and shrugged, then pointed to the blank areas on several retirement forms Keith had provided. "You have your mind made up. Why bother to counter Agent Benton? How much do you want me to accrue to your retirement funds, or do you want to follow up with HR? You left this part of the form blank, and I have no idea what's the percentages are that you've set aside over the years for your retirement portfolio."

"So, this is how you treat an undecided agent who may want to retire?" Keith had become angry at how Charlton was pushing him off. "You just sign away and—"

"Oh, so you don't want to retire?" Harris gave Keith a Cheshire cat smile. "I'm guessing you either want a transfer to that cushy New Orleans job that advertised interoffice memorandum, or..."

"Or what, sir?" Keith looked at Rachel grinning with a mischievous smile at Charlton. The two of them had a plan in play. And Keith narrowed his stare and smirked.

"Take a month off, Agent Benton. Paid. Lord knows after years of you never taking a vacation, you need it." Harris leaned forward on his desk and slapped his hands together as if that was final. It pretty much was.

"And just where would I be vacationing sir? Hawaii or New Orleans?" Keith unfolded his arms and pushed back his silver hair with both his hands.

Charlton leaned his head solemnly then lifted his eyes back up to meet Keith's eyes. Then he gave a slight smile. "Anywhere you want. But you know, I could use a guest in my private bungalow on Kauai, if you'll take the offer... from a friend. We go back a long way, Keith, if you can remember that far back. I know getting old is hell sometimes for veteran FBI superstars."

Keith crossed his arms again and leaned back in his chair with a chuckle. “That flattery won’t get anywhere with me, Charlton. I remember quite a few of our misadventures when we were partners. My senility hasn’t gotten the best of me yet. But I do wake up with more aches and pains these days in our golden years.”

Rachel rested both her arms on her thighs and added in, “Don’t we all wake up a little sorer and a lot slower these days, gentlemen? Obviously, it’s a result of our dedication to duty and from years catching bad guys in those wonderful mountains.”

“That it is, Rachel.” Harris cracked his neck and returned to his conversation with Keith. “Well, are you going to take the offer? Or will you retire or transfer? I wouldn’t transfer to the French Quarter if I was you, Agent Benton. Your old liver couldn’t take that kind of abuse these days.”

Keith barked out a laugh. “It’s great to know you’re always looking out for me, Director Harris.” He took a breath and looked out the window for a moment. He paused just briefly to watch both his bosses squirm—a little—waiting on his answer, which for him was obvious. He stood and shook Charlton’s hand. “I’d be a fool not to jump at that offer… Charlton. I’ll take the vacation at your private retreat and recover. When I get back, we can talk again if I’ll retire or transfer.”

“That sounds excellent my friend.” Director Harris returned the shake to Keith. “Rachel is right though. Now, more than ever, we need you.”

“I was being sincere, Keith. That wasn’t a pep talk, you know.” Rachel shook Keith’s hand as well and gave him a hug.

Keith put a hand on Rachel’s petite shoulder and admonished her. “Rachel, I know. But the time will come for all of us in the room to know when to pull the plug and finish our years enjoying the remaining time we have left. When the eyes aren’t working anymore, when the knees feel like burning gravel, when we try just climbing the stairs, much less running up a mountain, or we see our fellow agents fall—whether to bad guys or just plain poor health—maybe it’s time to let the younger agents take over. Let them fix our mistakes and make a few of their own.”

“Boy, that’s the most heartfelt and depressing speech I’ve ever heard from you yet. And that’s saying something.” Harris shook his head and pointed to his surfboard in the corner of the office near the coffee pot. “I think I’ll take the rest of the day off and go surfing to recover.”

Everyone laughed as Harris grabbed the surfboard and ushered everyone out of his office for the rest of the day.

Rachel fell into step alongside Keith as each went to their respective offices. “That was one of your most insightful and tear-jerking speeches to date. Please promise me that you will never give that one again. Unless it's my funeral. At which point I'll be dead and won't give a damn."

Keith shrugged and leaned in with a sheepish grin. "I promise, Rachel."

Walking back to his modest office at the end of the hall, Keith looked in on an auburn-haired agent with tired green eyes. She had piles of old cases stacked on her desk and three or four half empty coffee cups littered around her desktop computer. He thought of walking on and leaving the latest FBI superstar to her work. Then, he thought again and went in to give her some well-needed life advice.

Knocking on the glass door gently, he waited for the agent to usher him. As she did so, Keith gave a fatherly smile and asked, "How are we doing today, Agent Walker? Have you caught our latest baddie yet?"

"Oh, it's going. Just wrapping up loose ends on this one."

Keith chuckled. "I didn't ask how it's going. I asked how you're doing."

Agent Bella Walker groaned, leaned back from her desk, and gave Keith a wan smile. The look gave Keith all the information he needed to know. Bella shared his madness, too. She had that same obsessive, undaunting drive to catch a villain at all costs—marriage, health, and happiness be damned. He worried about her, especially now. One day if she didn't push the job away and relax, she might end up… well… just like him.

Keith walked in and sat in a chair across from her. He pointed to the stacks of cold cases and recent unsolved murders. "There will always be cases like these, Bella. There'll always be the one that wasn't found or got away. You know that, right?"

"I know. But I won't sit back without trying to at least make a dent. If we stick our heads in the sand, evil will prevail." She lowered her head and rubbed her bloodshot eyes.

Keith leaned back in his chair and crossed his arms. Lowering his head slightly, "I see that fire in you that's fueled me for a long, long time. I know that drive to catch criminals at all costs. You have that same madness I had when I was far younger and none the wiser. It's a blessing to the FBI but a curse to you living a normal, happy life. Keep bringing the work home, and there will be trouble."

Bella put her hands out in front of her desk and pushed back an open file. "And your reason for telling me this, Agent Benton?"

"I learned one thing when my wife died, Bella. Something that should have been evident from all the years working for the FBI." Keith sighed seeing that he had Bella's attention. "We are but specks of dust on this planet. A blink in this universe of ours at best. We toil and we stress, and we compete for what, exactly? At the end of it all, when our pulse stops, our bodies chill, and our eyes go gray and lifeless, what little happiness we found will blow away like the dust in our tomb. I've learned that happiness is all that matters, and all the rest is meaningless."

"Did anyone ever tell you, Agent Benton, that you have a way with words? Depressing as all hell, but quite a way." They both laughed then Bella continued. "How did you turn it off, master of the spoken word?"

Keith leaned in with steel eyes and a dour frown. "I didn't. And look how that turned out for me. Think it over, Bella, and learn from my mistakes. I lost precious years with my wife. And before I knew it cancer had taken the love of my life away. I felt cheated and angry for years, you see. But now—"

"But now what, Agent Benton?" Bella raised a brow and studied his next words.

"Now, I want to do it right this time, Agent Walker. I want to experience all this crazy world has to offer. I want to be loved by someone who will have me, and all my train-wrecked baggage." Keith smiled and stood to leave.

"That'll be one lucky woman to have you, Keith." Bella stood and patted his shoulder. "Lesson learned, sir. I'll leave the work at the office. I promise."

"Sure, you will, Agent Bella Walker. Try and bullshit someone else. We are cut from the same cloth." Both laughed again as Keith walked out Bella's door.

As Keith proceeded out, he heard a voice that felt like the piercing and irritating scratching of nails on a chalkboard. It was an ecstatic Director Harris whooping up a storm. "Agents, I need all of you in the conference room. A request for our services and help has been sent by Chief Thomas Kai of the Kauai Police Department.

Agent Keith Benton groaned. "So much for that vacation."

# CHAPTER TWO

***FBI Field Office***
***Enterprise St***
***Kapolei, Hawaii***
***October 10, 2023***
***10:40 A.M.***

Bella followed Keith into the FBI conference room. She sat next to her friend ASAC Rachel Gentry. She watched as Harris pushed the request form and file over to Rachel, who naturally placed it in Bella's hands. Bella winced and gave a sarcastic and sardonic grin at the sudden assignment.

"Well, this should be fun. I only have thirteen cases I'm working on currently in addition to this one," Bella grunted under her breath.

Bella read over the file as the rest of the team filed in. Harris moved to the front of the conference room and projection screen. He nodded to Rachel to launch the new case's presentation on the computer. Grimly he announced, "It looks like we have another serial killer plaguing our normally peaceful Hawaiian Islands. This time it's Kauai and Molokai where we are finding bodies. Several businessmen have been found dead floating in the Kauai and Molokai waterways."

"How do we know it's a serial killer, sir?" A tall, athletic Hawaiian man with raven black hair—Agent Billy Makani—asked earnestly. "This could be gang related or retaliation by local businessmen."

"It's a valid point, SAC Harris." Bella added in, knowing by her boss's demeanor he'd already vetted out that possibility. Charlton always triple checked before he made a statement. At his level of FBI upper echelon, he had to. "Maybe it's turf war fallout."

"We checked into that, agents. This is going to be a challenging case for the lead agent—that's you, Agent Walker. All these men are squeaky clean so to say. They all had powerful defense contracts with the military. Each was in their late fifties, and all were on their honeymoons."

"Well at least they got out of the bad marriages." A veteran agent with salt and pepper hair and a pencil-thin mustache—George Dwyer—shouted from the back of the room. Many of the agents laughed at his comic response. SAC Harris did not.

"You missed your calling as a stand-up comic, Agent Dwyer. Maybe I can arrange a gig for you." Harris glared at his warning which silenced the room.

"Sorry, sir." Bella heard George gulp at his boss's warning. "No disrespect to the living or the dead. It's been a few brutal months on these cases. I was just—"

"No worries, Agent Dwyer." Harris moved toward the projector screen a little closer. "We've all been a little tense with the increased workload lately. Anyway, the victims were all in their mid to late fifties, in good health, and there were no signs of struggle or trauma when the bodies were found." Director Harris pointed his laser pointer to each picture of the victims and the locations where they'd been found.

"And you are sure it's a serial killer, sir, if you don't mind me asking?" George had put his hands out flat on the conference table as if he were spreading a sheet on it. "You mentioned defense contracts. Could it be political assassinations? Someone who doesn't like the military-industrial complex?"

"I'm glad you asked, Agent Dwyer." Harris clicked to the next slide. It was a video of a woman paddling a kayak in circles on a slow-moving river. People in the background were shouting at her. She looked up from where she'd been paddling and leered angrily at them before suddenly seeming to flip a switch and start crying for help. "Now, it very well could be, depending on what the pattern ends up looking like. But KPD has a suspect at least for this murder. As you can see, it looks like an open and shut case for the late Alton Lincoln."

"They never are, sir, and you know that." Bella felt icy chills run down her spine as she saw the woman stare daggers at the camera. "She obviously couldn't overcome the deceased physically. And you believe there's a connection with her to the other murders in the waterways?"

Director Harris raised a puzzled brow. "Maybe, so, Agent Walker. She did kill this one on a waterway. But she looks nothing like the other brides of the other victims." He turned back to the video. "Chief Kai thought maybe there's a link, considering the similarities of the cases. But nothing stood out when he looked over the photos of the other dead men's brides. Plus, how any of them were killed still eludes us."

"Women typically—according to FBI statistics—kill their men with poisons. Were they poisoned maybe and dumped into the water?" Bella intuitively asked while looking back up at the picture of Alton's drowned corpse. The glare of the projector cast a dim shadow across the screen.

Director Harris shook his head then turned back to study the dead man's face. For a moment he paused looking at the screen. "Here's where KPD and MPD hit a snag, Agent Walker. Chief Kai was leaning toward poison as were the Molokai police. There was the issue of no trauma. Everyone thinks this crazed woman might be in some cult conducting rituals between both islands." He took a deep sigh. "But then the labs came back. Guess what wasn't in any of the men's blood?"

"Let me guess, sir." Bella looked down at the field labs sent over by Chief Kai. "There's nothing coming up on the toxicology reports to indicate poisoning."

"Bingo." Charlton rubbed his bristled chin, deep in thought.

"What about the cult theory then?" Keith pointed to Alton Lincoln's honeymoon picture and his bride. He took a breath then scowled. "Did anybody over on Kauai or Molokai think to detain and question the brides?" SAC Harris and ASAC Gentry both shook their heads at him. "Of course not. Why would I think they would? You know folks, this is starting to feel like the Jim Jones cult all over again the more I hear the details."

"I second that, Agent Benton. That was one horrific day, wasn't it." George put his right hand to his head and rubbed his temple.

"It was no picnic for sure. And I gave up drinking Kool-Aid after seeing all the dead cult members. To this day I can't stomach the stuff." Keith looked down at the table shaking his head in disgust.

"So, we go question the brides and detain them until one gives up the goods." Bella gave the ideal solution to wrap the case up promptly.

But of course, she knew there was a catch. There was always a snag when things were going too smoothly. It was evident in the way Rachel was looking at her with a sideways glance and as Harris put his hands out and shrugged. "Let me guess, they skipped town."

"Right again, Agent Walker. Each bride disappeared after the initial police interview." Rachel gave her a wry smile then added, "With skills like that you could have been one of those tarot card readers in the French Quarter."

Bella cocked her head sideways and rolled her eyes to Rachel. "Funny, Assistant Director Gentry. So, sir, I guess we'll be heading out to interrogate the witness that Chief Kai has in custody. The video evidence is certainly cut and dried for that one."

"Here's where it gets quite peculiar." Director Harris narrowed his eyes and gave a cryptic response. "The suspect—Candace Kincaid Lincoln—specifically requested you. She won't speak to any other law enforcement but Agent Bella Walker."

Bella frowned. "What?"

Harris leaned over the conference table and placed both his hands flat on it, giving Bella a stern glance. "Why would this suspect name you specifically? What's your connection to Candace Kincaid Lincoln, Agent Walker?"

Everyone stared at Bella with narrowed eyes. It was a jarring and unnerving feeling having her colleagues studying her like a lab rat. Her heart began to race slightly, and a light bead of sweat formed on her brow before she answered the boss's question. She fumbled through the file given to her trying to compose her thoughts, when something clicked.

"Hold on a minute," she said. She flipped through several files back and forth, rubbing her thumb and finger on her mouth as she considered it. "Yes.... Yeah, that's got to be it."

She jerked her head up. "Anyone got a pen?"

There was some surprised mumbling before someone passed her a pen. She immediately set to work marking and labeling the photos carefully.

Rachel couldn't hold back her curiosity. "What is it, Bella?"

Looking up at Harris and down the table to each of her fellow agents, Bella pointed to the pictures of the brides and then passed them to her team to review. She took a breath and wiped her saturated brow. "I have no idea why she requested me, sir. But I can answer one of our questions about her."

"And what question is that?" Harris sat down and leaned back as everyone else awaited her response.

Bella glossed over the photos one final time then spoke with certainty. "Each of these brides is the same one. Although prosthetics, hair style changes, and hair color were used to deceive us. This killer is a highly trained chameleon—maybe expert level training—with her deceptions. But if you look at specific features I have circled on each picture, you'll see it's the same woman. Whether it's a cult, I can't say. But I do know, she is the woman that killed all these men."

# CHAPTER THREE

"THIS WOMAN SPENT MONTHS, MAYBE YEARS GETTING TO KNOW these men. How she organized her relationships, duped these highly intelligent contractors, and timed these kills is quite extraordinary. It would take someone with the patience of Job, and the efficient expertise rarely seen in your average serial killer." Bella stood up and walked up to the screenshot of Candace Kincaid and her harsh, leering smile. "There's something off about this woman, no doubt. If she did kill them, her level of deception and ability to coordinate the kills is on a scale I've never seen before.

Rachel leaned in and stared sharply at Bella. "Well, that's saying a lot, Bella. You were almost killed by one of the most evil murderers of any century: The Harbinger Killer."

"That's correct, Rachel. He was on a Jack the Ripper scale of killing. But this one is different. Look at her face and the way she's positioned in the picture. She just married her brand-new husband, and this is her reaction? No guilt, no remorse, no sadness—until a split second later, when she has to pour on the tears for the cameras? It's downright creepy if she pulled this off."

Rachel rubbed her chin then added in, "Again, let's recognize she's just a suspect for now. While she may be the killer, I'm still finding it hard to believe she disposed of the victims alone in the dark on a remote waterway. And both these islands are remote with small populations of people. Somebody should have noticed an outsider with a body."

"That's the troubling thing here, folks. If what I've just read about the murders is accurate, this one would have gone on killing for years without being caught. Or has killed for years." Bella leaned back and took a deep sigh looking at Candace's picture. "This is a rare bird scenario, SAC Harris."

"How so, Agent Walker?" Harris raised a skeptical right brow.

"She let herself be caught, for starters. KPD didn't capture her." Bella pointed at Candace's face in the footage when she realized the bystanders had seen her. "Sure, maybe she hadn't expected it to end up this way... but a woman of her resources, who has apparently evaded everyone for so long now? No, I don't believe for a second that she got tripped up so easily. If she wanted to, she'd have found a way to squirrel out of the situation, just like she did every time before. But now..."

"Sir, this is a rare opportunity to interview a creature of pure evil. These are the type of killers we never interview, since they usually kill themselves before being captured. She has something to tell me that might be of use to the FBI. We need to honor Chief Kai's request and go to Kauai."

"Sounds good to me, Agent Walker. You and the team have fun out on Kauai. Harris, I need the keys to the bungalow so I can go on my vacation." Keith smiled and opened his hand as if waiting for Harris to toss him the keys right then and there.

Harris leaned his head down and raised his brow. "You'll get the keys to the bungalow and the yacht, as promised. But—"

"I already know, sir." Keith waved off Director Harris throwing him the vacation keys. He turned to Bella and shrugged. "What time do we all leave, Agent Walker? Looks like my vacation got put on a temporary hold."

Bella watched Rachel grin at Keith. Then she mouthed the words, "Thank you."

"Okay, team, it's settled. Get your affairs in order and close out any reports you were wrapping up before you leave." Harris turned to walk out of the conference room. Before he could exit, though, a man in his early thirties, with tussled, coarse brown hair and brown eyes timidly walked into the room. Harris winced as the strange man walked up and leaned into him to whisper something. Harris frowned. "Agent Walker, you and your team stay behind for a moment."

Bella walked over and nodded. "Sure thing. What do we need to talk about?"

Director Harris pointed to the disheveled, timid man who'd just walked into the room. While the man was a stranger to her, his name and the incredible work he'd done in forensic artificial intelligence techniques was not. "Agent Walker, this is Agent Victor Shelley. He's an FBI lab specialist from Quantico. He's—"

Bella excitedly interrupted. "You're the famed computer scientist who wrote the book on AI forensic techniques. Agent Shelley, that was amazing work using thousands of cross-sequencing probabilities to create high percentage outcomes for a murder suspect."

"Thank you, Agent Walker." Agent Shelley put out his hand to shake. Bella shook Victor's pale hand back as he added, "I am honored you read the old work."

Puzzled, Bella furrowed her brow and asked, "The old work? But that was just two years ago, Agent Shelley."

"The old work was boring, Agent Walker. But it was a fruitful endeavor that built trust with my colleagues. Those experiments allowed me to charge ahead with my new theories that will change the course of FBI forensics forever." Agent Shelley put his computer bag down and took out a small laptop for what Bella assumed was a presentation of his new work. "I think that after today, you'll agree."

"Well, you certainly have piqued my curiosity." Rachel tapped her fingers on the conference table and ushered Victor to proceed.

"On that note, I'll leave you fine agents to your new toy. Be safe on the flight out, team. Agent Walker, make sure to bring Agent Shelley back in one piece on this one. Use this valuable new resource any and every chance you get." Harris nodded to everyone and then turned and left the room.

"Yes, sir. We'll break in the new tech. Hopefully he can help," Bella replied as she took a seat next to Rachel and Keith waiting for Victor to begin.

Agent Shelley pushed back his tangle of hair before beginning. Straightening his shirt, Bella thought he looked more like a man about to raise a corpse up to the heavens for an electrifying resurrection rather than your ordinary FBI debriefing. It would turn out as Victor proceeded that she'd be right on both counts. "My team and I have worked on this project for several years. We are quite aware of the challenges each of you face as dedicated professionals for the Bureau. Long, tireless hours of monotony and speculation on every clue and scenario of a criminal."

Keith, not one to mince words or waste time, pushed the FBI specialist to hurry things up. "Thank you, Agent Shelley. Now cut the chit-chat and flattery and get to the brass tacks of why you are here. We have a plane to catch in two hours for Kauai. We will be interviewing a serial killer."

Victor lowered his pale head partially and narrowed his stare at Keith. "Interesting. That will be quite the experiment for the Ghost-in-the-Machine."

"The Ghost-in ... the what?" George moved his head back and widened his puzzled eyes.

Victor turned on his computer and linked it to the projector screen. Then he called up a presentation, showing Bella and her team a device that could have been just a pair of lightweight shaded glasses being worn by Victor himself next to a body surrounded by purple pulsing probes. "The Ghost-in-the-Machine is what I call it. I know with the pulse lighting, the corpse, and the lab guy wearing the glasses it looks like a techno DJ ramping up. But I assure you, this is an adaptive interface for communication using AI."

"Agent Shelley, could you say that in English for us non-scientist types," interrupted an athletic, platinum blonde woman with sky blue eyes—Agent Susan Namara. She rubbed both her temples and adjusted her glasses while taking notes.

"My apologies, agent. This is an artificial intelligence computing system housed in a pair of glasses. The Ghost-in-the-Machine virtual reality device uses mathematical probability and thousands of possible murder simulations from every killer the FBI has researched, caught, or killed. This device has the ability to think of how a potential killer might react based on these to assist in the investigation. It runs through millions of statistical scenarios and possibilities to account for any possible missed factor when it comes to an investigation." Victor adjusted his glasses and nodded to each of the team to make sure they understood.

"So, it's a high dollar probability sleuth." Agent Makani leaned back in his chair and raised his brow.

Agent Shelley stood stoically with his hands lowered and held in front of him. He seemed to be readying himself to explain. "In some ways, that is correct, sir. But in the most important element of our development of the machine, that's the tip of the iceberg."

"How so, Agent Shelley?" Bella shifted in her chair and put her hands together as if praying. She asked the question on everyone's mind. "You did mention an adaptive interface for communication using AI."

"That's correct, Agent Walker. Let me explain." Victor clicked to the next slide which showed pulsing, vague images. "I created this machine not just for probability. It reasons as the victim might have reasoned, using all the background information it can find or be given. We put in every facet of information pertaining to the victim's life. Their history, their background, their social media, their statements from friends. It cross-references this information with the psychological profiles of thousands of other victims. The end result is, well... the device thinks like a victim, it reacts like a victim, it *becomes* a murder victim—or the murderer, when asked. My machine—using AI science—talks to the dead."

The whole room seemed stunned by Victor's bold statement and the video of his revolutionary device.

"How can we be sure it's accurate at all?" Rachel asked, breaking the overwhelming moment. "Certainly, we can't use the information to build a case or put away a killer in court. I'm sure it's a helpful tool, but we can't just assume that this... machine knows what it's like to be human."

"No substitute for good old fashioned police work. Done by a man," chimed in George Dwyer.

"Or a woman!" Bella admonished him. George held up his hands in defense of himself.

"Now Agent, I didn't mean it like that. I meant the generic sense of the word. Man... or woman. As opposed to a machine, that is. A human."

Victor looked at the group and nodded. It was obvious that he had heard this argument play out many times before. "That is the next frontier of this research. While, of course, I can't guarantee the results of my algorithm, I'm working tirelessly to make it as accurate as possible, so that we can someday trust the results with the utmost accuracy."

"Well, I don't know about the rest of you, but I just got the creepy chills seeing this thing work in a presentation," Keith admitted. "Thinking like our victims to solve their murders is one thing. Having this toy—which is no toy but a Pandora's Box which we probably shouldn't open—imitate them or the killer freaks me out, man. I'll probably leap out of my skin if we actually use it."

Rachel didn't miss a beat with her own sarcastic retort. "You probably would, Agent Benton. It wasn't that long ago when I was holding your hand when you got scared watching Michael Jackson's 'Thriller' video.

Someone—either Susan or Billy—started singing the song behind Keith.

"That's not funny, knuckleheads. Y'all know I don't like scary movies." The whole room erupted into laughter and singing as Keith grumbled something to make a zombie blush.

***Oasis Airline Charters***
***1004 Bishop St***
***Suite 2719***
***Honolulu, Hawaii***
***15:00 P.M.***

Two hours later, Bella sat in the latest Honolulu charter flight lobby—Oasis Airline Charters. The plush seating was a far cry from the rock-hard seating of their many flights across the Hawaiian Islands. The extra padding and crispness of the leather was a welcomed surprise of comfort. Seated between Susan and Billy, Bella took in the various trendy magazines and the two large, screened TVs in front of her putting out the news cycle from two different corporate organizations twenty-four hours a day and seven days a week. She glanced up, making a brief mental note of one news story in particular about a recent scandal at the defense contractor Yellowrock. Apparently, several of their latest experimental craft and weapons hadn't been up to the Pentagon's standards.

Bella grimaced as the reporter droned on.

*Why am I not surprised there's another defense contractor scandal. These Pentagon guys spend trillions on weapons and technology that they know will fail. If we could use five percent of their annual budget to improve impoverished communities or update infrastructure, we'd change all the hostility in the world. Most certainly we'd end these stupid, endless wars.*

"Bella, isn't that the dead guy?" Susan pointed to the right screen on the TV. The announcer was discussing the recent contract between Raylight and their Yellowrock top consultant Alton Lincoln.

Bella narrowed her eyes and rested her chin on her right hand studying the story. "Yes it is, Agent Namara. Which makes this case even more of a headache. We'll have to follow up with his employer if no one has told them already that he's been killed."

"I'm betting they already know, Agent Walker." Keith sighed and looked toward her with a concerned brow. "These cases—especially defense contractors—are never just cut and dried. Let's hope the guy wasn't embezzling from his employer and really just on his honeymoon with a black widow."

"If I never hear that name again, I'll be forever grateful. We've had enough spiders in my lifetime, Agent Benton," Agent Namara added as Billy looked over and comically shook to get rid of bugs. Everyone chuckled except George. He was napping in his chair.

***Lihue Airport***
***Mokulele Loop***
***Lihue, Hawaii***
***October 10th, 2023***
***17:20 P.M.***

An hour later, the plane made its final circle to descend onto the island of Kauai. Just before the descent at Lihue Airport, Bella took a sip of water and studied the terrain that they'd be investigating for the next couple of days. Throughout the trip, Bella took in the remote, verdant jungles and mountain peaks as they made their descent. She recalled how powerful and overwhelming the scents of plumeria, sandalwood, and jungle had been on her last investigation to capture General Arkar Sai—the man known as The Spider, and his accomplice, the crazed Sasha Conan—the Black Widow. Now, they'd be way south of that case to the eastern point of the island and further inland.

*Hopefully,* Bella thought as she looked out on the vast winding expanse of the Waialua River the site of the latest murder. *As long as I don't have to climb through anymore river-soaked lava tubes or blast my way out of any coastal caves it should be fine.*

The heat, and the humidity from a recent rain, felt oppressive as the FBI team stepped out of the plane. Bella put a hand up to block the glare from the tarmac despite wearing sunglasses. Waiting with two tinted black Escalades was an athletic, Hawaiian man with salt and pepper hair wearing a cowboy hat and police uniform—Chief Kai.

He smiled broadly to Bella and everyone and put his left hand out to usher them to the vehicles. "Welcome back, agents! It seems just like yesterday we had three hundred people scrambling all over Waimea Canyon looking for a spider."

"Don't remind me, Chief Kai. My shoulder still hurts on cold rainy nights from his minion's bullet." Bella groaned as they moved to get into their FBI vehicles.

Inside everyone was updated on the latest with Candace Kincaid. Bella noted Chief Kai hesitated and adjusted his cowboy hat before delivering the news. Grimly he gritted his teeth. "She's escaped."

George leaned forward and wiped his mustache. "What do you mean she's escaped, Chief Kai? You had her in a locked room in handcuffs."

"We did, Agent Dwyer. I swear she was cooperating and ready to spill the beans to you, Agent Walker. I have no idea what happened after I left. Somehow, she got the jump on my officer and used him as a hostage to get the keys and run off into the jungle. We scanned with forty men to find her. We lost her trail just west of Kealia Forest Reserve."

Bella darted her eyes to Chief Kai suspiciously, "Who was the officer? How long has he been on the force?"

Rubbing his shoulder and looking over to Bella briefly, Chief Kai answered. "His name is Robert Kapaa. He's been one of my go-to guys for the last three years. He's a loyal, dedicated, and tough as nails professional, Agent Walker. He's not the kind of guy who makes mistakes like this. Robbie's one of the few who wouldn't take a bribe."

"And yet, a woman with the physique of a long-distance runner got the drop on him. A woman in handcuffs, I might add, chained to an interview desk," Billy growled skeptically while crossing his arms.

Chief Kai flushed with obvious embarrassment. "Well, not exactly handcuffed."

Bella and everyone shook their heads in disbelief. Then Bella inquired, already knowing the answer. "Are you telling me that you let her out of the handcuffs thinking the interview room would hold a serial killer in check? No worries, I can see by your face, you did. Let me also guess that because she was small and hardly the size of a gazelle, she posed no threat. I'm imagining Deputy Kapaa is a powerfully strong man, an intimidating man, and just the officer who would keep her in line. There was no way you thought little bitty, poor little Candace Kincaid wouldn't try anything to escape."

Shaking his head red-faced with shame, Chief Kai admonished, "Even the best of us, Agent Walker, screw up sometimes. Luckily, she didn't kill my stupid deputy or anyone else."

"You mean yet, Chief Kai," Billy added angrily. "She didn't kill anyone else, yet. With her track record, there'll be another murder soon."

Everyone agreed, including Chief Kai. Sighing he explained his latest plan to find and catch her. "Moving forward from this colossal screw-up, I believe that she'll be involved in another murder, Agent Makani. Which is why I have organized over sixty personnel, spread out across Kauai hunting her down. I also got with the harbor master to close all the ports and report anything suspicious. Same goes for the taxis, rental cars, and ATV places as well as the airports. We are doing everything to block her from escaping. Hopefully, it's enough to buy us time to catch her."

Bella patted his shoulder then gave him a stern look. "It's a good plan, Chief Kai. But I'm going to recommend hauling in Officer Kapaa for questioning. Don't let him out of your sight for sure. I want to interview your deputy after we check into the Sheraton. I want to see if there's anything she might have indicated as to why she escaped."

***Sheraton Kauai Coconut Beach Resort***
***Front Desk***
***650 Aleka Loop***
***Kapaa, Hawaii***
***18:30 P.M.***

Bella's team's black SUV pulled up to the vaulted front entrance of the lush Sheraton Kauai Coconut Beach Resort. Surrounded by coconut palms along Kauai's eastern coast, the enormous facility looked like an extravagant compound of condominiums to Bella. As they unbuckled and stepped out of the vehicle, Bella looked up to the towering black wood awning that was intricately carved with traditional Hawaiian artistry. She heard the sway of the green coconut palms and smelled the charring of tiki torches or a luau grill somewhere in the distance.

Walking up to the front desk with Chief Kai and her team, Bella took in more sights of laughing people and hand carved curiosities before checking in. As they strolled up to the desk, the manager of the hotel waved to Chief Kai.

The man who was dark skinned and held a pleasant smile advised, "Chief Kai, your office has been trying to reach you." Chief nodded and went to make a phone call while Bella and everyone went up to check in.

Bella had just finished getting her room key and was looking forward to a nice hot bath when Chief Kai stopped everyone with some important news. "Agents, my people , have located Candace Kincaid."

Excited with the news, Bella spoke in a rapid flurry. "That's great news! We need to make sure she's handcuffed on the ride back toward the station and triple guarded. We don't—"

"She won't need handcuffs or guarding anymore, Agent Walker." Chief Kai took off his hat—a rare thing—and spoke solemnly. "She's dead."

# CHAPTER FOUR

"WOW, WHERE'D SHE KILL HERSELF?" BILLY MAKANI BROKE THE silence. Everyone hurried and climbed back into the Escalade headed out to the crime scene.

While everyone was shocked by Candace Kincaid's untimely death, no one was really surprised. Statistically, from the FBI database, capturing a living serial killer was a rare event. Most killed themselves or were killed when trying to capture them.

But then Chief Kai advised how Candace's body had been found. Pointing in the direction of the mountains north of them. "She was found floating face down by a kayaker doing some early morning fishing. The man said it was the creepiest thing he ever saw."

"What was so creepy about finding a body?" Rachel said sarcastically and rolled her eyes.

"I know, dead bodies are always creepy. Anyway, Cesar—that's the guy's name—said the fog was billowing off the water and at first, he thought she was a dead fish brought in by the tide. Thinking her a snagged carcass, he was about to paddle away. Then, he got a closer look and realized the 'fish' was a blonde-haired woman. He called us immediately."

Chief Kai then pointed in an easterly direction where a thunderstorm seemed to be erupting in the distance. "The location they found Candace was where the Anahola and Kaalula Streams meet up just west of Anahola Beach and Kahala Point. Once again, there's no signs of trauma or a struggle. So—"

***Kauai County Medical Examiner & Coroner***
***3-3420 Kuhio Highway***
***Lihue, Hawaii***
***19:00 P.M.***

"You think she killed herself with her own poisoning?" Bella interrupted and watched Chief Kai shake his head as he parked his vehicle at the morgue.

"I think so. But here's the problem I'm having, Agent Walker." From behind the wheel, he pointed to the thunderstorm moving fast across the jungle toward them. "She was positively identified in the northern part of Kealia Reserve. I had thirty men tracking her that swear they caught sight of Candace running ahead of them, near to crossing the rivers northwest of the reserve six hours ago." He rubbed his temples and seemed to stare hard in the direction of the Kealia Forest Reserve. "Even if she'd hidden an ATV, or hell, a rocket ship, in the reserve to escape, there's no way she'd made it from that dense jungle to Anahola Stream in six hours."

"I agree, Chief Kai. That would be impossible to do even with an offroad Jeep. I know, I tried it on a few occasions when I lived here." Keith uncrossed his arms and nodded in agreement. He and the rest of the team unclicked their seatbelts and stepped out of the parked vehicle.

Bella huffed, shaking her own head. "The logistics are always a nightmare on these Hawaiian islands." Bella turned to Agent Shelley who had been quiet and observant to everything going on. To Bella he seemed to have a Sherlock Holmes-like style of watching, analyzing, and then keeping things close to his chest.

Bella shrugged and ushered him forward.

*There's no better time than the present to see if his gizmo actually works. Or if it's just another highly touted and overpriced dud turned out by the FBI.*

Bella pointed to Agent Shelley who had moved up to shake hands with Chief Kai. The tired police chief shook hands back warily. "Chief Kai, I want you to meet Special Agent Victor Shelley from one of our experimental labs in Quantico, Virginia. He has a new device that might be able to help us this round."

"Sounds great, Agent Walker. What's he need from me?" Chief Kai half smiled and nodded to the forensic scientist.

"A body." Victor said icily to Chief Kai who widened his eyes in disbelief.

"Well, the way this case is going, Agent Shelley, there should be plenty to feed your monster." George added as lightning crashed outside illuminating his face like some laboratory henchman from a Universal movie.

Candace Kincaid's body was pale and lifeless in the Kauai Morgue. Ironically, it was placed on a cold steel table next to the man she'd killed twelve hours earlier. To Bella it was a macabre, sad scene seeing the dead husband and his heartless killer bride together again. She shuddered a moment before following Victor, who moved like a lightning bolt setting up the electrodes and gadgets for Candace's brain.

The team sat back studying Victor's process for setting up the Ghost-in-the-Machine. Susan in particular turned her head sideways confused and asked, "You're hooking up a virtual reality computer on a dead woman. How are you supposed to extract any information from a dead body, Agent Shelley?"

Agent Shelley stood back and checked several signals with a device that seemed to measure sound waves or something else. "It's simple enough, Agent Namara, once I'd mapped out the process. Honestly, like a lot of breakthroughs, it was blind luck. I was working on another project I called 'Forest God Pan' when the solution for this one came to me."

Curious Susan raised her left brow to ask. "How's the device record?"

Victor adjusted the purple strobes of two of the probes and typed in several notes into his laptop. "That device hasn't been built yet. We've been throwing around several theories—AI simulations, Many Worlds theory, quantum graviton measurements—""

Susan, unimpressed and more confused, shook her head. "That's cool and all Agent Shelley. However, the Ghost-in-the-Machine is what I'm asking about. *How* will it communicate with the dead?"

"And I was getting ready to tell you, Agent Namara." Victor seemed a little annoyed by Susan's impatience and interruptions. "Have you heard the saying 'the eyes are the window to the soul'?"

Susan shook her head that she hadn't.

Bella intervened, "I have. But what's that got to do with this machine, Agent Shelley?"

"Everything. It'll make more sense inside. Basically, you'll see three to four possible outcomes simultaneously of what could have happened to Candace Kincaid, based on all the information we have available regarding the circumstances of her demise. Once we input the data, it should provide us with every forensic possibility. Well… that's the hope, anyway." He linked a nearby monitor with what looked like a specialized internet booster then turned on the screen. After completing the link-up, Victor Shelley handed the special sunglasses he had discussed in the earlier presentation to Bella. "You're the lead agent on the case. So, it's logical you get to be the first field agent to use the glasses on an actual case. The first time you go into the void—that's what we call the pre-simulation—it'll take a few minutes to adjust. You may vomit or become disoriented. That's a normal response."

"That's wonderful to know, Agent Shelley. Does anyone else want to be the guinea pig and make history?" Bella offered the glasses to everyone. All shook their heads and passed on the offer.

"Forget what you know of time. Forget everything you've researched on psychoanalysis. What you've been told about ghost memories and post-traumatic stress disorders, or recurrent nightmares, will pale to what you are about to experience. If there's any doubt or fear to proceed, I'll totally understand and take over the simulation. Do you understand?" Victor produced a waiver for her to sign just as he turned over the glasses.

Bella gave him an icy stare. "A waiver, really?"

"Really." Victor pointed to a cocktail of medications near the chair Bella would be sitting during her trip into Candace Kincaid Lincoln's dead mind. "I'll have a sedative ready and the emergency room has been contacted in case there are complications. It's a mandatory protocol. No one really knows how a living person will respond to being killed in their mind over and over again. What you feel, what you see, and what you experience will be recorded in the software and by the digital devices I've set up. It'll be invaluable data."

Bella pressed her lips in a tight line. "Glad to be of service."

Victor took a deep tense breath, "Are you ready?"

"Let's get this over with, Agent Shelley." Bella nodded and looked at her team. "If he messes my mind up, shoot him." She smiled wickedly as Victor nervously gulped. "I'm kidding Agent Shelley. Besides, I'll shoot you myself."

"Remember it's all a simulation and not real. If you get overwhelmed, pull off the glasses or shout 'stop'. I implemented a failsafe with the word 'stop' that shuts the whole system down."

Bella nodded to indicate that she understood and put the glasses on. "These are just like reading glasses." Bella felt the sand-colored rims slide snug over her ears and heard the click of the device turning on.

Immediately, Bella felt as though she were being pulled through a swirling vortex of twisting, star-filled space. Her stomach twisted as if she were on the worst rollercoaster of her life ascending to the heavens, only to be pulled and shook right and then left with the force of a train car braking sharply. In the moment, Bella couldn't help it, and fell from the chair she'd been sitting in and threw up. In the distance, as if a wayward echo, she heard Keith and everyone ask if she was alright. For a moment with all the swirling and twisting, she wasn't. But then she was able to raise a hand and say she was okay. Two sets of hands put her back in the chair. But the hands, like the voices, felt like hands moving her underwater.

Bella heard the voice of Victor Shelley as she slowed into what was an abyss that was dark as night. It was a darkness occasionally illuminated by arcs of blue and purple lightning. In the blasts she looked down at what she perceived to be her hands and body. They too gave off a shimmer and opaque look as if underwater. Bella waited and drifted in the dark waters preparing for the machine's next move.

It wasn't long before the Ghost-in-the-Machine pushed Bella's mind forward into several AI recreated moments of Candace's life. Each always starting with the sight and scent of plumeria flowers falling over her head in torch lit darkness. After which, Bella felt herself dancing away the evening with Alton to Wayne Toup's version of "New Orleans Ladies." Each time Bella wanted to cry, seeing and feeling that joyous moment between Candace and Alton especially as they sang along together.

Somewhere in the distance, she heard Victor's voice saying that they'd gotten all the details straight from Candace's account, down to the plumeria flowers. It looked so unbelievably real.

She felt the powerful arms of the dead man, breathing deep to waft in the warm musk his Givenchy cologne. She could even taste the salt in his lips as they kissed. Then each time she saw Candace in the mirror of the bathroom alone as Alton went to get ice. Except in the mirror—she was Candace!

Bella didn't hear Candace's thoughts. She felt them.

*I will kill him because he hurt me long ago.* And she did.

The scene shifted and once again, she was back at the wedding. The whiplash was jarring. The song played once again. They kissed. They danced. They kissed some more.

*I will kill him because he is an evil man.* And she did.

The scene changed once again. Each time, Bella's thoughts and stomach lurched. The whiplash from the anger and rage to the happily wedded bliss almost threatened to send her falling out of her chair once again. She danced with Alton, knowing she had just killed him. Knowing she would kill him again.

She looked down to see blood staining her pristine white dress. But a blink, and it disappeared. Of course. There had been no blood at the scene. That was just her own mind playing tricks on her.

She kissed him, she killed him, she started it all over.

Bella felt Candace's angst and saw her rage at being forced to kill Alton. Her orders were clear—eliminate the target. But four tear-filled, agonizing times and she had refused. Her handlers swore they'd kill her if she botched the murder again.

*I love Alton. I will kill myself instead. But they will still kill him regardless no matter where he goes.*

As the machine progressed to the sixth or seventh simulation—Bella had lost count and fully given herself to the whims of the machine—she became the dead woman's thoughts.

*If they make me kill him, I'll kill all of them in return. I'm tired of their games.*

Bella pulled back from being Candace. Then in a last heave to find out who the 'they' were, she dove back deeper. This by far was the worst, and Bella almost vomited again. Candace had been poisoned at this point and Bella felt its effects. Her skin was on fire as if in a roasting oven. Her brain arced flashes and also had caught fire. In and out of a delusional spin, Bella felt Candace's terror as she realized the terrifying truth.

*These useless sacks had the nerve to kill me with my own cocktail!*

Candace's heart was sputtering like a ripped balloon as she tried in vain to stop the shadowy men from dragging her off into the jungle. She knew—Bella knew—in those final moments Candace was dying. Candace and Bella felt the pull and heard the splash as both were tossed like a bag of garbage into the waters of the stream. She looked up to the vastness of the starlit cosmos and smiled.

*I'll be with Alton soon if he'll have me. I hope he understands that if I hadn't killed him, someone far worse would have. Why didn't I just come clean? We could've run off and hid somewhere.*

The waters were cooling her and there was hope in each of her deaths that the dose might have been too weak, and she may live. But then the fires would return, making her blood boil and her head would ache. It was then she pushed herself beneath the cool waters just as Alton had gone beneath the cool waters. She bobbed up only once, seeing a sign that said Anahola Stream before taking a final spasmed gasp and dying. This is how Candace's death played out each time the Ghost-in-the-Machine ran through her final moments.

"Stop!!!" Bella screamed, shutting down the simulation. It could have been its eighth run or its eighteenth, she could no longer tell. She fell to the floor, threw off the glasses, and pulled herself up into a ball sobbing uncontrollably. She screamed "Stop!" a second time, hitting both sides of her head for a moment before lifting her head realizing the simulation was over. Taking in deep, controlled breaths, she calmed herself and focused her mind.

Victor Shelley bent to one knee to help her up. He reached down and grabbed Bella's arm roughly to get her to stand. As he did so, Bella rocketed her left leg and knee into his midsection. She cracked him a second time with a scissor kick to his gut dropping the man in a gasping heave.

"Bella!" Billy shouted. Rachel ran to her aid while Keith and George helped up the skinny Victor.

"Are you sure you're okay, Agent Walker?" Keith had helped Bella walk out of the morgue and as far away from Victor Shelley's dangerous machine as was humanly possible.

"Ask me in the morning, Agent Benton. Right now, I need to clear my head." Bella gave a wan smile and nodded to him. She looked at the concerned faces of everyone. Of course, they were concerned after what they had all witnessed.

Agent Shelley, rubbing his bruised gut, went to speak. "Agent Walker, I can't begin—"

Bella was abrupt and growled, "Can it, Dr. Frankenstein! We can talk about your experiment and everything tomorrow. Right now, however, I need to get this woman's ghost out of my head. No more talk about that damned machine."

No one said another word on the ride to the hotel.

# CHAPTER FIVE

***Sheraton Kauai Coconut Beach Resort***
***Front Desk***
***650 Aleka Loop***
***Kapaa, Hawaii***
***21:00 P.M.***

TWO HOURS LATER, EVERYONE WAS DROPPED OFF AT THE SHERATON Kauai Coconut Beach Resort for a much-needed rest. That went triple for Bella Walker. She was still coming down from the Ghost-in-the-Machine's effects. And the comedown in some ways was worse than being inside the simulator itself. Distinguishing her real life from the ghost woman's life was nerve-wracking. After two grueling hours, she still carried Candace's memories and feelings. Walking through the lobby of the hotel, Bella felt her fiery rage of being betrayed and killed.

Climbing into the elevator with the FBI team, she could still taste the salt of Alton's warm lips as they danced their first dance as husband and wife. Candace's lingering feelings of anger, of coldness, of sadness, of fear, of overwhelming love made Bella want to punch her hotel door as she fumbled with the key. And in the quiet and chilling cold of her lonely moonlit room, a waterfall of heartbreaking tears fell from Bella's face, feeling the weight of the doomed couple's lives.

After three hours of silence and thinking, Bella realized the worst and most twisted thing of all. This cold-blooded assassin had fallen deeply in love with her target, sealing both their fates. She was not your typical garden-variety serial killer. Especially if what Bella had felt and seen of the woman was true in her final murder.

Running through all the possibilities, all the scenarios, all the repetitions, Bella somehow knew that there was more to the story than simple revenge or deception. She didn't discount the possibility that it might have been, but even in her thorough research of Alton Lincoln's past, she hadn't been able to find anything that fit that pattern. For that matter, it didn't account for why Candace had killed so many other victims as well.

What had united them? They were all men, of course. They were all defense contractors. But what made Alton different?

What made Candace want to come forward this time? But then, what changed? What made her want to escape? To kill herself?

Was Candace a political radical? Someone so deeply committed against the military-industrial complex that she took it upon herself to personally assassinate so many of its members? Did she do it on behalf of an organization? Had she been ordered to do this?

Bella turned all these questions over and over in her mind, remembering how the Ghost-in-the-Machine had processed every possibility of emotion for each of these scenarios. She reviewed her notes and double checked the case files of each murder as memories of Candace's life washed over her.

"You truly loved him, didn't you?" she asked in the empty room. "Whatever your flaws, whatever your true intentions, you loved him. You didn't want to kill him because you loved him. That was why you stayed behind. Why you turned yourself in. You were going to tell me everything."

The explanation rang true in her mind. It was as if Candace herself was nodding to her.

"But what changed, Candace? Why did you run?" Bella leaned back and closed her eyes. "Who chased you?"

*My employers,* came the immediate answer. The mental voice was an uncanny mix of Candace's and her own.

"But who are they?" Bella asked. "What did they ask you to do?"

No answer came this time. The Ghost-in-the-Machine was a marvel of technology, but it could not truly read the thoughts of the dead. It could not provide information it didn't already have fed into it in some way. Candace's true motives remained a mystery, one that she would forever take to her grave. But even though Bella had briefly been a facsimile of her, she felt like she was already putting things together in her mind.

Candace had been ordered, despite her pleadings to these mysterious employers, to kill the man she had loved. And Candace knew with certainty that her refusal had doomed her.

*Lady, you were one cold-blooded killer. But I must admit you certainly were fearless and selfless in the end. The strangest feeling of all is that you were fine with dying. Especially if dying meant you could be with Alton again. There in the void, I could see your final thoughts as you submerged beneath the black waters.*

Or at least an approximate estimation of her thoughts, anyway.

The phone rang, bringing her back to reality. It was SAC Harris. Bella pictured him at home sitting back in his creaking chair. "Bella, I heard from Victor Shelley. You had quite the haunting from his toy."

Bella walked to her fridge and pulled out a lemon water. Twisting the cap with her right thumb she chugged the whole bottle. She had never done that before. "I am still having quite the haunting still, sir. That machine is no toy. I felt everything Candace felt. And saw everything she saw, sir. It was, well, mind-blowing."

He chuckled softly. "Glad I opted out of testing it then." Harris seemed to be sipping his own drink on the other side of the line. Bella could hear the rattle of ice in his glass. "The reason I called is I need all of you back here for a team debriefing. I especially want to hear your insights on our serial killer."

"She wasn't a serial killer, sir." Bella fired back defensively. Parts of Candace's thoughts were still affecting her.

There was a pause on Harris's side of the phone line. Then in a gruff voice he demanded, "Say that, again, Agent Walker. Your voice sounds a little testy and defensive. Are you sure you're okay?"

Bella sighed and shook the vestiges of Candace from her brain. "Sorry, sir. I'm still having a hell of a time sorting everything out. But reviewing the evidence, as well as the circumstances of her death... I don't believe she was a serial killer. Not as we traditionally define them."

Harris harrumphed. "Well then, what was she?"

"I believe she was an assassin, sir."

All Bella heard for a long moment was the clink of ice in a glass. "Sir?"

"Interesting," was all Harris finally said. "Do explain, Agent Walker."

"Every victim she killed was a prominent defense contractor. She had specific methodologies and specific methods. But what gets me the most is... I believe that she truly loved Alton Lincoln. I saw her thoughts and felt her pain. I experienced her wedding day, just as she described it. It was beautiful."

"Don't tell me you're going soft on me now, Bella."

Bella smiled. "Nothing of the sort, sir. I just mean that Mr. Lincoln was a unique circumstance in all her killings. She really loved the guy. She didn't want to kill him, but she was ordered to. That was why she allowed herself to be caught. Why she was going to turn herself in... until she mysteriously disappeared. I don't believe she ran away to escape arrest. I believe that her employers, whoever they are, extracted her, knowing she'd spill the beans on their entire operation. And they neutralized the threat to them."

"Frankly, Agent Walker, my first instinct is to say you're talking crazy. But with some of the cases we've dealt with lately..." he took another sip of his drink. Bella idly hoped it was root beer and not whiskey. Though she doubted it. "I don't know it'd surprise me much these days."

"The question is *who* are her employers? Could she be some hard-core anti-war activist committed to peace by force? Could she be connected to organized crime? Lord knows we've had enough of those cases lately..."

"Could she work for another corporation? Bumping off the competition?" Harris asked.

Bella chuckled. "Now who's talking conspiracy crazy, Harris. But it's as good a possibility as any. Unfortunately, as brilliant as that Ghost machine is, it couldn't give me any specifics."

"I want you to get checked out back here when y'all fly back tomorrow. And don't you dare go near that machine again! I'm going to be sending Agent Victor Shelley back to Quantico after the meeting. That machine is way too dangerous for anyone to use right now in the field. It might help us solve crimes faster, but it will all be in vain if we wreck the minds of our best agents."

"I guess that's a compliment sir?" Bella snickered, feeling better with each passing hour.

"Don't let it go to your head." Director Harris roared with laughter at his pun. Then he warned Bella again. "I didn't like what I saw his machine do to you on the video feed, Bella. Maybe we aren't meant to know so much about killers or their victims. We've done pretty all right for ourselves with old fashioned intuition, investigation, and speculation."

Bella tossed her second bottle of water into the trash can. "No worries, there, sir. I'm not going anywhere near that Ghost-in-the-Machine again."

"I definitely believe you on that one, Agent Walker." Director Harris sounded like he moved forward in his office chair. Bella could hear him tapping his fingers on something. "I'm starting to think Keith was right. The world really is a crazy place these days."

"Don't tell me you're thinking about retirement too, sir. A spring chicken like you?"

Harris barked out another laugh. "Funny, Agent Walker. But the time may come when Agen Shelley gets enough of those machines out into the field to put old detectives like me out to pasture."

"I think that day is a long way away, sir. After all, a machine can't bribe people to stay in the Bureau with a vacation house." Both laughed heartily again. It was the kind of laughter Bella needed after such a horrific day.

"I know this will be a tough one after what you've been through today, Agent Walker. But I need you to ship both Candace and Alton's bodies over to Oahu for follow up analysis with our new lab."

"No problem, boss."

"I'll see you and the team when you get back." Bella heard the phone line click off as he hung up. The sound was similar to the Ghost-in-the Machine clicking off. She fought off a mild urge to throw up.

***Lihue Airport***
***Mokulele Loop***
***Lihue, Hawaii***
***October 11$^{th}$, 2023***
***10:00 A.M.***

By ten A.M. the next morning, Bella and the rest of her team were back on board their charter plane flying with their iced precious cargo—Alton and Candace Lincoln. Bella, looking out over the shimmering blue ocean from her plane window, was feeling loads better. Her head had cleared of the ghost of Candace after a few hours of sleep.

"Welcome back, Bella. We noticed you had quite the possession." Rachel, to break the ice, and ease the tension joked. Bella rolled her eyes then cast a glance toward Agent Shelley.

"Funny, Rachel. Maybe Agent Shelley can send you on your own journey into the mind of a dead woman." Bella pointed over to Victor who was distracted in deep thought.

Rachel narrowed her eyes and looked toward Victor. "No worries, I'll pass. One scrambled FBI brain—though Agent Walker probably didn't have much up there to stir up—is enough. I heard you took quite the kick."

"It wasn't Agent Walker's fault. It's quite common for there to be outbursts from the subject when the machine is unplugged," Shelley replied. He seemed to be taking it well, considering everything. He took a slow breath and continued while guarding his stomach with his right arm. "The whole team can vouch though. The machine exceeded all our expectations."

"So, we all heard, Agent Shelley." Rachel turned back to Bella as everyone climbed into the FBI gray escalade for the drive to the office. Pulling her aside, she whispered, "As your best friend, Bella, don't you ever use that crackpot's invention again."

Bella half-lowered her head and whispered in return, "No worries there, Rachel. I never want to get near that brain sucking machine again." Then she pointed to the two bodies being placed in the coroner's van. "I guess we'll be working with the new coroner to figure out the poison Candace used on her victims."

"No, you won't be working with the new coroner. Harris made a few phone calls. He found us an FBI biochemist with a specialty in poisons." Rachel went around to her door and got in. Bella, after placing her bag in the back, climbed in on the passenger's side.

"That'll work. What's his name?" Bella clicked into her seatbelt and adjusted her armrest.

Clicking in her own seatbelt and putting the vehicle in drive, Rachel answered, "His name's Dr. Larry Wecht."

Bella asked as she looked over to Rachel. "Wasn't he head of the forensics department of Quantico? I never knew he held a biochemistry degree and specialty in poisons. I just took him to be—"

"The morgue guy." Keith interrupted. "Everyone makes that mistake about Larry. But you'll never meet a more dedicated and driven scientist. Well, except for Agent Shelley. I'm guessing you have some fancy doctorate, too."

"Yes, but I hate being called a doctor, Agent Benton." Shelley leaned back with the sun casting its glare across his pale face. "I have my master's in biochemistry as well. But my doctoral dissertation was in neurological mapping of the brain."

"Well, that explains everything." George adjusted his seatbelt as Rachel drove into the parking lot of the Hawaii field office building.

"Oh, it does, Agent Dwyer?" Shelley sat up and prepared to unlock his seatbelt to exit the vehicle.

"Yes, it explains why you are a bona fide nutcase! I ain't ever going near that brain scrambler of yours for sure!" Laughter erupted throughout the vehicle as Agent Shelley smirked.

***FBI Field Office***
***New FBI Morgue***
***Enterprise St***
***Kapolei, Hawaii***
***October 11th, 2023***
***11:10 A.M.***

Conveniently for the team, the new morgue was in the rear of the FBI building. The building's new, dark gray paint had recently dried. But the masking tape was still present on its front windows as Bella opened the door to step inside. She'd brought Victor, Billy, and Susan to tag along and take notes should they find something with the pathology, and toxicology reports.

A tall, red-bearded man with a slight stomach paunch, and salt and crimson hair was thin slicing organs for slides from Alton Lincoln. He wore brilliant blue scrubs, a clear face shield to protect his blue eyes, and a morgue apron. He looked up to the agents who'd just interrupted him. "Can I help you?"

"Dr. Wecht?" Bella asked as she looked on the body of Alton with mixed emotions. She became a little shuddery from seeing the dancing man carved up. She still felt the kiss of his lips from Candace's memories.

"Yes. And by the look you are giving the deceased, you must've had history with him. Who are you?" Dr. Wecht stopped his pathology slices and raised his face shield.

Bella began introductions and pointing. "I'm Agent Walker. This is Agent Makani, Agent Namara, and Agent Shelley. We—"

"Agent Walker, you got this nutcase out to Hawaii?" Dr. Wecht pointed to Victor. "Don't tell me, Agent Shelley. Someone finally gave that abomination of a machine of yours a round. I've warned you too many times, Victor, you shouldn't be playing God with the dead. Those things have repercussions. Just read 'The Great God Pan' by Arthur Machen to see how that turned out for them. You dabble too recklessly with the nature of things that you barely can comprehend."

"And yet, Dr. Wecht, we had a major breakthrough with the Ghost-in-the-Machine just yesterday. Agent Walker was able to pull from the deceased killer's memories her motivation for killing the man you are cutting up." Victor gave a knowing grin and pointed to Alton.

"Is that true, Agent Walker?" Dr. Wecht almost seemed disgusted by the news.

"In a certain sense," Bella amended. "The machine itself allowed me to see and feel what could have been her last moments. But it was only with my human mind that I was able to start to truly progress the investigation."

"Much is still to be done with refinement," Victor said excitedly. "It is of course still a work in progress."

"Well, I don't recommend ever using that machine again on anyone. Its effects are quite unnerving." Bella walked over to look at Alton's surgically cut up cadaver. Then she glanced timidly over to Candace's covered corpse and shook her head. "So where are we on the latest toxicology and pathology findings?"

Dr. Wecht took off his gloves and removed his face shield. "This one has stumped me, folks. Candace Kincaid had to be one of the best poisoners out there for me to find nothing after three hundred organ slides, and ten toxicology lab runs. If I was to guess, she had some biochemistry training or was a specialist herself. Are you absolutely sure she poisoned all her victims?"

"If her memories reviewed eight times by me in her skull are accurate, Candace admitted as much." Bella pursed her lips and narrowed her eyes toward Victor.

"I checked his stomach and went inch by inch checking the intestines. I thought I'd find something there." Dr. Wecht removed his apron and sat in a chair near the body studying it. Leaning back, he placed his bearded chin to rest in his right hand. "All I found was a bunch of medicinal physics nuts."

"A bunch of physics nuts? How many did you find?" Billy Makani asked curiously. He moved closer to look at the organ table where the Hawaiian plants were.

Bella looked over at him puzzled. She too moved next to him to look at the seeds. "Is there something you want to share with us, Agent Makani?"

Billy looked over to Dr. Wecht who had stood and also moved to the organ pan next to Billy. "I'll know for certain, once I get my answer."

# CHAPTER SIX

"THERE WERE AT LEAST THIRTEEN NUTS IN HIS STOMACH, AGENT Makani. Is that significant?" Dr. Wecht furrowed his brow studying Billy.

Billy counted all the seeds that had been spread out by Dr. Wecht. "More than three have enough ricin to kill a full-grown adult unless they are cooked. By the look of these, they weren't."

Dr. Wecht nodded. "Makes sense. It would be almost undetectable by normal methods."

"In some of our traditional legends, our dark magic practitioners often used numbers to signify the reason for killing. In this case, I believe they might have killed him over something to do with war," Billy said.

Bella crossed her arms and looked over to both bodies again then back to the seeds. "So, the number means that Candace killed him because of a war. And given that he—and all her other victims—are defense contractors, that makes sense. It definitely puts me in the thought process that she's some sort of anti-war activist."

"But enough to kill these men in such a brutal fashion?" Keith asked. "Political violence is one thing—but for her to pose as a wife, to deceive and seduce these men, and then kill them… to me, that's a hell of a lot more personal. That's not a political method—and in any case, it's not very efficient."

"Right? If she wanted to kill a bunch of war profiteers, there are way more conventional ways to do it." It was Susan who said this, to the surprise of many. "Most political protesters would make some big show of it, trying to get their cause on the media and bring attention to it. But she didn't do that. She killed these men practically in secret."

"Good thinking, Susan," said Rachel. "So she's maybe not a committed activist herself, but an assassin working at the behest of… who?"

"That's the million-dollar question, Rachel. And I'm betting, by what I felt in her last moments, she might have been poisoned, too," said Bella.

"By what you felt of her last moments?" Dr. Wecht looked over to Victor who nodded. "You can't take anything you felt with that machine of his as gospel, Agent Walker. The signals may have induced a condition that might have felt like her thoughts. But in the end, it could have been you were projecting what you thought Candace Lincoln might have felt. Hence, why I told that knucklehead he needs more testing and better control groups."

"I took your advice to heart, Dr. Wecht. But that's why I'm here. I've got to get field data from some of the Bureau's top investigators to help train my artificial intelligence algorithm."

Dr. Wecht shook his head. "Reckless. Unnecessary. Just look how it's affected Agent Walker. How long were you plugged in, agent?"

Bella shook her head and shrugged. "I don't know, Dr. Wecht. My understanding of time got all twisted up. How long was I plugged in, Agent Shelley?"

Standing across from Alton's surgically cut corpse, Agent Shelley answered as he looked down at a sewn -up surgical incision on the body. "Two minutes, Agent Walker. Most of my trial personnel only lasted thirty seconds before they had issues."

Wide-eyed in outrage, Dr Wecht exclaimed, "Dear lord, Agent Walker! What the heck are you doing back on the job after that kind of scrambling?"

"I got a follow up this morning, Dr. Wecht. I'm fine. I couldn't say the same thing yesterday as Agent Shelley found out." Bella gave Agent Shelley a stern glance. The agent rubbed his midsection where Bella had launched her kick.

"Well, if you start having any audio or visual... moments, you get your butt back into the hospital. You got it?" Dr. Wecht pointed at her forcefully. It was apparent he wasn't persuaded by Bella's insistence that she was totally fine.

"I do, Dr. Wecht. You have my word that I'll go running if their ghosts come back." Bella pointed to the two bodies. Then she turned to her team. "Billy and everyone, we need to hit the databases on this plant. Candace might have used more than one plant to get her targets to ingest the ricin. Dr. Wecht, how could she have got them to eat these seeds?"

Dr. Wecht shrugged, "If I had to guess, since she knew her stuff about plants, Candace might have eased them to their deaths. Some sort of hallucinogen. Agent Makani, what plant can you think of in the jungle that could bring about a hallucination?"

Billy's eyes went wide with disbelief, and he put his hands out defensively. "I don't know, Dr. Wecht, Hawaii only has a few thousand of those. But if I was a betting man—since Candace was time-limited—wood rose. There's a sea anemone that is way more powerful, but it would've taken her a week to hike and swim to it."

"Thanks, Agent Makani. That gives me a clearer understanding of how she poisoned her victims." Dr, Wecht glanced over to Bella and offered a hypothesis. "She worked them up and slipped her hallucinogen to them, most likely in a drink. Then in their relaxed state, Candace fed them poison. But how she was able to time when these victims would die was quite extraordinary. She somehow managed to leave the bodies perfectly clean of any poison afterward. Leaving them with no trace of the true cause of death. She certainly was adept in her coordination. Until she met Alton and got sloppy."

Bella took a sigh as she looked over to Candace. "There were complications with this murder, Dr. Wecht."

"And what were those, Agent Walker?" Dr. Wecht asked as he went over to his laptop to research the FBI poison database for the team.

"She fell in love." Bella turned and nodded for everyone to leave the busy mortician to his work.

Four hours later, Bella, Billy, and the team had looked over thousands of poisoning cases involving plants across the globe, with a special focus on the deaths of defense contractors. This was easier said than done, of course, because they quickly found just how interwoven the web was.

"Wait, Raylight has a subsidiary that manufactures car tires too?" Billy groaned. "We'll never get a comprehensive look at all these contractors. Much less all the deaths of all their employees."

"Add it to the list, Billy. Susan is looking up the solar panel division of Advanced Mechanics and George is looking up a recent acquisition of Bedrock Consolidated that builds elevators and escalators."

"They make air-conditioning systems too," George chimed in helpfully.

"At least they're not blowing hot air," cracked Keith. Everyone laughed at that, which provided some much-needed levity before they returned to their work.

Meticulously, each had poured over the records looking for patterns or links to their current case. Then Bella cross-referenced the FBI pharmacological database regarding hallucinogenic plants that could have preceded their deaths. None of the cases seemed to follow any particular pattern that Bella had hoped to find.

Victor groaned and threw a file in disgust. "This is getting us nowhere. Any number of killers could have used any number of combinations of poisons to kill."

"That's the reality of the job, Agent Shelley. Murderers come in all types. It's difficult wading through and finding links. We can't all climb into the minds of the dead for our answers." Agent Namara smiled at him and pushed back a lock of her blonde hair.

Billy leaned back in his conference room chair and put his hands behind his head. "Yes, even field jobs can be boring and tedious when we're on the hunt, Agent Shelley. As Agent Namara noted, murderers come in all types—"

"And from different countries." Bella grinned at her team as Rachel walked in to bring everyone out to lunch. "We need to see where the victims came from and the specific plant that killed them."

Agent Shelley walked to pick up the thrown file. Then he turned with a knowing grin. "You're thinking, what I'm thinking aren't you, Agent Walker?"

Bella stood and grabbed her purse and ushered everyone to lunch. "It's a theory at best for now, Agent Shelley. But if the specific class of poisonous plants are regional in each murder, we better understand how she was killed. After lunch we'll follow up with Dr. Wecht."

***Spammy's Grill***
***Honolulu, Hawaii***
***October 11th, 2023***
***13:00 P.M.***

"This is the Big Kahuna jalapeno ghost pepper spam burger. It's a rite of passage for Hawaiian FBI agents visiting the island." Billy slid the congealed ham-like burger over to Agent Shelley and smiled.

Agent Shelley raised a brow as he studied the monstrous sandwich. "It looks like a walking heart attack burger to me."

"The peppers should offset any inflammation. But I'm sure your cholesterol will go through the roof." Agent Namara grinned wickedly at the pale-skinned agent.

Rachel shook her head as she took a sip of her green tea. "Okay, gang, let's get to brass tacks. What's the plan moving forward, Agent Walker?"

Bella put down her own ghost pepper spam burger and answered by wiping mayonnaise from her mouth. "I want each of these countries followed up on. Agent Makani, you take Myanmar and check out these one hundred and fifty poisoning cases. Agent Namara, I want you to tackle these one hundred and forty cases in Bangladesh. Agent Benton, I have you focused on Thailand and these two hundred cases. Agent Dwyer—"

"I know, Agent Walker. The rest are mine." George gave a half grin and groaned.

Bella tried to be diplomatic. But everyone knew George was the fastest and most efficient record reader and closer on the team. "Well, I subdivided it into four major countries—Nigeria, Egypt, Colombia, and Dubai. You are one of the best we have at going through these quickly. It's only five hundred files."

"No worries, Agent Walker. But you know I'll probably find a few thousand more that match her methods." Everyone nodded in agreement.

***FBI Field Office***
***New FBI Morgue***
***Enterprise St***
***Kapolei, Hawaii***
***October 11th, 2023***
***18:00 P.M.***

Bella left the team reviewing piles of records and making phone calls to other field offices trying to identify and cross-reference any victims that fit the pattern—whether they were from Candace personally or, to her own horror as she was discovering, from a network of highly-trained killers all using the same methods. In just their preliminary follow up poison cases, a dreadful connection was coming to light. Bella needed to share it with Dr. Wecht and get his opinion.

"Dr. Wecht?" Bella watched as the pathologist made notes in his laptop on the latest lab specimens he'd reviewed from Alton and Candace. "Do you have a minute?"

"It depends, Agent Walker." He looked up and narrowed his tired eyes at her. "Do you have a breath mint?"

"That's kind of an odd request, Dr. Wecht. Why do you need a breath mint?" Bella looked at the man puzzled and crossed her arms.

"Oh, the mint isn't for me. It's for you. That smell of pepper on your breath is killing me." Larry let out a howl of laughter as Bella's face went flush with embarrassment. "Great, now my eyes are watering." He laughed even harder.

"That's just great to know my breath is killer." Bella tightened her face and murmured, "Is everyone around here trying to be a comedian?"

"Sorry, Agent Walker. As you know in this business, with all this darkness and death, you have to keep a sense of humor." He shrugged and pointed to his lab findings. "Seems like you were right on the poisoning being the same for both. I'm glad you called me on your theory. Were there others elsewhere that were like this?"

Bella took a breath and nodded. "Yes. There are more cases we've possibly to her method. She was a brilliant killer that would never have been caught using her techniques unless she wanted to be caught. And what's worse is they were all around the globe. All the cases point to her use of rare plant poisons, native to whatever region she was working in, and not just isolated to Hawaii. That was a lot of travel for your not-so-average killer. Whoever paid her travel bills had deep pockets."

Dr. Wecht crossed his arms. "No one would be looking for a rare or not-so-rare plant poison when the toxicology would be limited in its scope. We can admit that Candace must've had a tremendous understanding of each country's lab capabilities or lack thereof."

Bella walked around the bodies and looked back to Dr. Wecht. There was still a lingering connection to Alton and Candace's last memories that Bella found unnerving. It was as if she was expecting both to sit up and have a casual conversation with her as if she were a long-lost friend. "There's only one thing that concerns me, Doctor, and it's a big one: what if Candace isn't the only one?"

He looked at her over the top of his glasses. "Are you thinking of a copycat?"

"I'm thinking of a highly-trained squad of assassins. Some organization out there is training women in the use of rare plant poisons and unleashes them on the world."

He grunted. "Troubling indeed."

"And that makes me concerned that, if this organization is operating in Hawaii, with direct knowledge of this case... they may try to cover their tracks by any means necessary. Is there any way that my team can protect themselves?"

"In all these emergency poisonings, Agent Walker, the most important thing is to stop the histamine cascade. That is when a reaction—allergic or otherwise—occurs. You have seconds to shut down the massive release of vasodilators from the mast cells and basophils. There's really only one thing that blocks the cell fast enough to interrupt the leaking."

"And what's that, Dr. Wecht?" Bella had walked back over to look at Dr. Wecht's computer screen. But before she reached him, he had projected the answer on a screen behind her.

Dr. Wecht turned the model of the drug and showed how it worked on a human cell. "Epinephrine. It's faster than diphenhydramine or any of the corticosteroids. It works in seconds rather than hours like the other two. Load your gang up with a few epi-pens and you might actually save a life one day." He clicked a button and projected the medication up on his own large screen with the drug's chemical formula and molecular shape. "I pray you never need to use them though."

"You and me both."

# CHAPTER SEVEN

***Bella Walker Bungalow***
***Nimitz Beach, Hawaii***
***October 11th, 2023***
***20:30 P.M.***

BELLA HEARD THE WHIR OF HER SECURITY GATE OPEN AS SHE PROceeded to drive up the winding road to her bungalow home. As she parked, Bella waved and called out to two familiar faces who came out of her home. One was her beloved Alaskan husky Thor. The other was the love of her life—Justin Trestle, better known to some as the "Conjure Man" for his uncanny nature. The latter had saved her life on a snowy mountain years ago, when the Harbinger Killer had done his worst.

"Who's a good boy?" Bella fell to play with her excited dog as Justin set him loose.

"How was your trip?" The six-foot-five giant of a man gave Bella a knowing smile, then cast a look of concern at her.

Bella put her head down and grimaced. *Somehow, he knows what happened in that morgue on Kauai. I suppose he is the Conjure Man... or maybe Keith Benton texted him. That's probably it.*

"I'm never volunteering for another FBI brain scrambler, if that's what you want to know." Bella walked up and gave her boyfriend the most passionate kiss of his life. She watched as Justin studied her intensely right after. "What's wrong? You look concerned, honey."

Justin pushed back slightly to look deeply into her eyes. "That's the first time in all the years we have been together that you threw one whopper of a kiss on me in public. Not that I'm complaining, that is."

Bella looked around with a chuckle. "The driveway ain't exactly public."

He scoffed. "You know what I mean. Now, something happened with that machine and your brain. You're going to tell me everything that happened with that brain scrambler. Or I'm taking you to get a second medical opinion from a doc I know who specializes in former MK-Ultra victims."

"It wasn't MK-Ultra techniques, Justin." She could see that they couldn't just stop at a vague conversation this round. "Fine, sir. This special agent—Agent Victor Shelley—hooked up electrodes to the brain of a murder victim. The victim we thought had been a serial killer. But it turns out she might be some type of assassin or murder-for-hire contractor with expertise in poisoning."

"Okay, so how did you get chosen for this machine? And how long did that whackjob have you hooked up to it?" He and Bella walked hand in hand into the house while Thor barked and followed in tow.

"No one wanted to try the machine. So naturally, being the lead agent on the case, I volunteered." She saw Justin wince as she said the word 'volunteered'. How many times had he preached to her the tried-and-true real slogan of the Navy? *Never Again Volunteer Yourself* had been spouted countless times by Justin and every one of his current or former Navy colleagues while they had been together. She rolled her eyes at him. "I already know what you are thinking of saying. Let's skip that part of the preaching."

"I didn't need to say the motto, Bella. But by the looks of things, next time heed it." Justin brought two plates of food from the kitchen and placed them on the dinner table.

Bella looked down at the pineapple smothered chicken topped with some secret pepper sauce that Justin refused to give the recipe to. The meal was her favorite dish. "Wow, you went all out tonight. I know it's a tactic to get me to gladly spill the beans. I say mission accomplished."

Bella took a lemon water that Justin had placed with their meals, quickly popped off the lid, and hurriedly chugged the water. She was wiping her mouth and was about to dig in when she stopped herself.

Justin was wide-eyed in disbelief. Thor had his head cocked sideways confused at his momma's odd drinking behavior. Both looked at each other. Justin shrugged to Thor. And Thor barked something that only Justin could understand. Then both turned back to her as Justin spoke a warning. "Every detail, Bella Walker. Or we are going to see the MK-Ultra shrink."

So, Bella told him every detail no matter how insignificant. She described the machine itself. She explained how Agent Shelley had hooked it up on the dead woman and herself. Bella told Justin of the side effects she had been warned about, the contingency should she get overwhelmed, and most importantly to Justin—what the whole experience felt like.

She described her tumultuous emotions of seeing someone else's life flash before her eyes. Of loving, killing, and dying. And then waking up to do it all over again.

In the end he stayed quiet for almost half an hour thinking. The latter aggravated her to the point where she finally broke the silence. "Well, do you believe me?"

Justin opened his mouth as if to finally say something, but he paused. She was about to scream at him to say anything, when he spoke. "Yes, I believe your brain got racked pretty good. Whether it was your projected thoughts or a dead woman's last minutes, well, it's a bit of a stretch, in my opinion." He put his hands up to pause her from pushing back. "But, I'll admit, it could be possible with the advances we have made in neurological mapping of the brain. But to be honest, it's hard to get my head around all this stuff." Justin gave her a big smirk on his play with words.

Unamused, Bella slugged her boyfriend a good one in his tree-trunk sized arm. Then she growled, "Hard to get my head around it… you'd better believe me mister. Or you can sleep in Thor's doghouse tonight."

Justin stood and walked toward the door. "Well, on that note I believe you wholeheartedly, Bella. But I have to take a raincheck tonight on staying over. The package has arrived, and I have to get things ready back at Trestle Castle."

"Are you talking about what I think you're talking about, mister?" Bella narrowed her eyes and stood crossing her arms.

"Yes, the full animatronic dragon kits have arrived. We are going to have full scale dragons hovering over the castle moat!" Justin's eyes lit up. He was as excited as a young kid getting their first model plane or train set. "And the fog machine and propane fire effect pack lets them billow out fire."

"I just got back from getting my brain scrambled in the skull of a dead woman. I explain I feel like I'm having her ghosts in my memories, and you want to run off to play with a bunch of dragon toys." Bella huffed and stomped her foot. "Do you see the problem here?"

"I do. That's why I pushed the delivery until next week." He gave Bella a mischievous grin. "I just wanted to check how you'd respond to me leaving. And you certainly didn't disappoint, girlfriend."

"You can skip the cute psychoanalysis, Sigmund Not-Freud. And you aren't my boyfriend much longer." Bella gave her own wicked glance as Justin moved in haste back to the living room where Bella ordered him to the couch. She relished watching the towering giant nervous and edgy. And that had been her plan for quite some time with her soul mate.

"What does that mean, Bella? You aren't breaking up with me over the dragon gag, are you?" She could hear Justin stuttering nervously a little over his words.

With Justin seated and tense, Bella sat nearer to him and leaned her head on his shoulder. Then she whispered in Justin's ear, watching the hairs on his neck stand up as his skin flushed on his neck. "I think the time has come to talk about our future, Justin Trestle. I'll let the Conjure Man figure out what I want from you. And... how he *proposes* to do it."

Bella heard a deep gulp from him and giggled. He was about to say something when the phone rang.

"Who is it? You're breaking up on the line." Bella stood to get a better signal. She tried to focus her hearing and moved to putting her finger in her other ear to block out any additional distracting noise. The tactic helped a little. "Is that you, Aunt Natalie?"

Justin mouthed the words, "Aunt Natalie," then made a shame-on-you expression rubbing one of his index fingers across the other. Bella gave him a warning stare that his joke wasn't funny.

"It's great to hear from you, Aunt Natalie." Hearing her aunt's voice picked up her spirits after a long grueling day. "How have you been?"

"You can cut the small talk, Bella." It was typical Aunt Natalie wanting to talk, but not wanting to waste her words on idle chit-chat. Bella grinned at Justin and shrugged as Aunt Natalie continued. "I don't have long to chat as I'm between flights. I just wanted to call and let you know I'm on my way. Tell Algernon it'll be good to catch up."

Puzzled by her aunt's cryptic message, Bella asked the all-important question. "You're headed where, Aunt Natalie? I thought you were going on vacation to the Himalayas."

The phone line became choppy. Bella figured Aunt Natalie must be boarding her next plane as her aunt answered. She was quite surprised by her aunt's next words.

"I'm headed to vacation in the Himalayas after we wrap up this case."

Bella's pulse took off like a freight train with palpable excitement. She was getting the opportunity to come full circle in her career! She and Aunt Natalie would work together to solve a case. "That'll be great Aunt Natalie!"

Both Justin and Thor cocked their heads sideways, perplexed. But Bella paid them no attention. "Have you ever seen anything like this?"

Bella heard a pause on Aunt Natalie's side of the phone. Then she heard someone with the flight team ushering Aunt Natalie onto the plane. Then she heard the same flight person apologize to her aunt for not knowing she was an FBI agent. "Bella, were the male victims on a honeymoon? Also, were the men previously abused husbands?"

Bella furrowed her brow and walked to the bay window looking out on a starlit sea. "Well, our interviews and reports indicate that our victims—well, had been abused by their previous wives. Yes, they were on their honeymoon. But their current marriages were happy ones."

"Hmmm, that's very... curious, Bella." There had been a pause. It was an obvious cryptic ploy that her aunt was using to stall what she really wanted to divulge. For whatever reason, Bella felt Aunt Natalie was holding a key to help her case. Then Aunt Natalie confirmed her suspicions when she blew her off. "Nothing comes to mind, Bella. We can talk more about the case when I get there. The plane is fussing me to get on board. See you soon."

Bella wasn't letting her aunt off the line that quickly. "Hold on, Aunt Natalie! I know that trick works on Mom and Dad. But not on me and especially not on a case this twisted. You know something, I can feel it. Help me out here so I can follow up on the lead before someone else gets killed."

"You're too smart for your own britches sometimes, little lady," Aunt Natalie fussed. "I'll level with you, Bella. I've seen this before. There was an assassin back in the mid-nineties and early two-thousands who killed defense contractors. Each man had been in an abusive marriage with a spouse, divorced after years of legal fighting, and then remarried. I came close to catching her out of Kuala Lumpur but somehow she got tipped off and got away. I never figured out her identity and only knew her code name as Sure-Kill."

"Sure-Kill," Bella whispered. "Pretty ominous name."

"That it is, Bella. That's why your boss called me in on this one. Anyway, I have to get off so the plane can take off. We'll talk soon."

Bella pressed her lips in a tight line. She was excited by the prospect of working with her aunt, but for SAC Harris to just call her in without even so much as informing her was irritating. "Alright. See you soon!"

Bella hung up and settled back into the couch. "Sure-Kill… Sure-Kill," she whispered.

"You alright there, Bella?" Justin asked.

"Have you ever heard of a killer code-named Sure-Kill, Justin?"

He shrugged. "Can't say I have. Not my area of expertise."

"Well, that's a shocker. And I thought you knew just about everything."

"Just a little bit about just about everything," he replied with a grin.

Bella ruminated through the information her aunt had provided her. Surely Candace Kincaid Lincoln was not one and the same as this Sure-Kill? If she was, she'd been active far longer than Bella had thought.

Which only served to make this case even more impossible to figure out.

"Who knew there were so many defense contractors that got divorced after terrible marriages?" she wondered aloud.

As if answering her Rachel groaned sleepily and yawned out, "Agent Walker, we found another businessman floating in a river. It looks like he's been dead awhile and most likely a victim of our dead poisoner."

"But she's dead," Bella protested.

"May have been before. May have been after. Or…"

"Another killer," Bella groaned.

Rachel yawned a second time. "I'm scrambling to schedule flights now. I'll call you when we get them together. We'll probably be leaving in the next four hours for Molokai. Advise your team to be ready then get a nap."

"Sounds good." Then Bella almost forgot in the moment an important additional passenger. "Oh, Rachel, you'll need an additional seat for an arriving forensic specialist who has experience with our lovely assassin."

Rachel seemed to growl awake at the addition of a new agent to the team, and the hassle of booking a new flight on short notice for the mystery agent. "Agent Walker, is there something you want to tell me before I book that ticket?"

Bella's pulse was back in overdrive with excitement relaying her great news. "Well…"

# CHAPTER EIGHT

***Oasis Airline Charters***
***1004 Bishop St***
***Suite 2719***
***Honolulu, Hawaii***
***October 12th, 2023***
***02:30 A.M.***

"THIS SEEMS LIKE OLD TIMES, BELLA." RACHEL TOOK A LONG-tired breath and handed Bella a cup of black coffee. "You, me, and the team waiting in another airport to go to another crime scene on another dangerously remote Hawaiian island."

Bella yawned and took a sip of her coffee. "Why, what's it been? Forty-eight hours?"

"I would have thought forty-eight weeks," Rachel said.

Bella looked over at her friend with concern. "You've been sleeping much since you took on the new job?" The question was rhetorical. Bella could see the bluish bags under Rachel's eyes. They told Bella all she needed to know. Rachel looked like she hadn't slept in a month.

"You already know that answer, Agent Walker. But rest assured, I'll catch up on my beauty sleep on the flight over to good old quiet Molokai." Rachel took another sip of coffee, then leaned in her chair thinking. She hesitated a moment before adding, "That island usually never has things like this. The local people are usually very quiet and law-abiding. It's sad when some outsider goes there just to wreck the peace and tranquility."

"The taking of a life anywhere can do that, Rachel. But yeah, I'm tired of these killers coming to our happy place and ruining it. I take these murders personally, as you know." Bella took her own sip of the bitter black coffee then looked over to the rest of her team. Everyone, with the exception of Agent Shelley, was fast asleep in their chairs.

"Anytime someone wants to murder on your island, or murder you, it's beyond personal, Bella." Rachel looked out to the tarmac. She watched as their plane was pulling up and being fueled. Then Rachel turned a glance toward Victor. "What's the deal with that one? He's as pale as a ghost himself. Maybe that's why he's so fascinated with ghosts, Bella."

Bella leaned over to mention to her friend. "Maybe so, Rachel. I know that the name he gave to his machine is spot on. The Ghost-in-the-Machine was totally accurate at what it does. I swear Rachel, Candace Kincaid's memories and emotions buzzing around in my noggin felt like her ghost possessed me. And that was hours after the machine was off my head. I tell you Rachel, I truly believe we aren't meant to break the natural order of life and death."

Rachel looked onward to the plane. The lead flight member was ushering the FBI team to board. Both women stood as Rachel ushered Bella to the plane first. "I believe you there, Bella. But I see the machine's promise, too. You got to see what Candace was like in the flesh. Her memories. Her emotions. Her dreams. And that's even if it might have been your subconscious projecting what you thought she would be like. Powerful is an understatement for that kind of victim or criminal insight. Some might call it a spiritual experience." She snickered as Bella turned around and glared.

Running into the charter flight main room with her overnight bag gripped firm, a woman who was the spitting image of Bella—with a few extra years on her—sprinted up to the team. "Looks like I got lucky and made it just in time, niece."

Wide-eyed and in disbelief seeing her Aunt Natalie actually before her, Bella said the only thing she could in the moment. "That you did, Aunt Natalie."

Aunt Natalie gave a warm grin in the direction of Keith. Then jokingly chided him. "Well, there's a relic of a face I haven't seen in a long time. Charlton hasn't fired you yet?"

"I begged him to retire me. Then demanded him to fire me, if you recall that conversation." Keith grinned over to Aunt Natalie and shrugged. "So, the other day I asked for the transfer we spoke about in New Orleans. You know the job, Agent Roberts. I was taking your old assignment as you had retired, ma'am."

"Let me guess his counter-offer. He wouldn't take your resignation. Then he gave you the FBI morale speech or pushed it off on one of his underlings. When that wasn't working, he hedged all bets and pushed for you to take a vacation at his personal bungalow." Aunt Natalie looked at Bella who pointed to Rachel. Bella saw her aunt realize she had just made her first gaffe.

"By Agent Walker's pointing and your eyes, I see you were the underlying that our fearless leader pushed off said morale speech to." Aunt Natalie watched as Rachel narrowed her gaze and nodded. "Well, I'm Agent Natalie Roberts. And you are?"

"I'm ASAC Rachel Gentry, Agent Roberts. But I'll answer to 'underling' if you like." There was a tense moment between Rachel and Aunt Natalie. Bella was shocked by both agents behavior.

Then laughter erupted between them, to the utter bewilderment of Bella. Then the rest of the FBI team with the exception of Victor Shelley burst into laughter. Bella groaned. "You guys got me good! I should have known."

"It's been too long, Rachel. How's the family?" Aunt Natalie winked at Bella who shook an accusing finger at her aunt and Rachel.

The team moved quickly to board the chartered jet for Molokai. Rachel updated Aunt Natalie as they went to sit in their seats. "Dad works too much, and Mom worries… too much. But everything is going well in the international banana operations. We can't keep up with the cattle and macadamia nut demand though." Rachel clicked into her seatbelt then added, "You caught us all off guard flying out here. I thought you were going on vacation in the Himalayas."

"I was, Agent Gentry. But then I heard that my ambitious but foolhardy niece went and scrambled her brain on that mad scientist's latest field-approved invention." Natalie gave a pointed look at a nervous Agent Shelley.

Victor put his hands out defensively as he sat in his seat. "Agent Roberts, despite your protests about the Ghost-in-the-Machine and trying to scrub my projects, we had a breakthrough. Bella lasted longer than anyone. She—"

"She could have irreparable damage from that mind poke you did, Agent Shelley. This was the main thing Dr. Wecht and I warned you about. How the brass approved you to take it out in the field with it after all the initial negative testing, I'd like to know." Aunt Natalie put her hands slowly together and looked up sternly trying to read the scientist's response to her statement.

Victor locked himself into his seat then explained. "I re-ran the tests four more times, Agent Roberts, with controlled timings of no more than one minute. The results of the studies were so encouraging, Quantico cleared us for a field trial. Agent Walker's courage to volunteer—"

Wide-eyed and exasperated in learning Bella had volunteered to use the Ghost-in-the-Machine, Aunt Natalie scolded, "Isabelle Lauren Walker! You volunteered! You never volunteer for any half-baked FBI experiments ever. Didn't I warn you repeatedly not to ever volunteer for a suicide mission?"

Bella calmed herself before answering. She was already starting to regret working with her equally bullheaded and ambitious aunt who had made her own mistakes for the FBI science division. Bella recalled one of her aunt's misadventures involved lysergic acid tolerances should an agent get dosed by a bad guy. But rather than kick off a ruckus with her aunt in front of the team, Bella cooled her jets. She looked around at the team snug in their plane seats. Then, as she heard the plane revving the engines and felt the movement of the jet heading out for takeoff she answered Aunt Natalie. "Yes, you did, Agent Roberts. Sorry."

Bella leaned back in her seat and closed her eyes. She had decided she'd better cat nap on the forty-minute flight. Pulling her own airplane pillow behind her head, she thought, *I need the twenty winks. Who knows when I'll sleep again, the way this case is going.*

***Molokai Airport***
***Island of Molokai***
***Hoolehua, Hawaii***
***October 12th, 2023***
***03:35 A.M.***

Bella dreamed of towering black cliffs that rose out of a churning white sea. She smelled the powerful aromas of pungent jungle earth and all manner of tropical flowers. Then she opened her eyes from her nap as the jet touched down and landed. Molokai exceeded all her Hawaiian Island dreams.

The mountains seemed to tower beyond the halls of Heaven itself on the island of Molokai, covered in lush jungle and greenery. The fragrances of plumeria, coastal sandalwood, and other flowers of Kauai that had so overwhelmed Bella were even greater in this remote paradise. And Bella reminded herself these overwhelming island fragrances were from just stepping off the plane. Then as she and her team navigated on the remote red dirt roads to get to the Molokai Police Department, the vast isolation hit her. It would be a logistical nightmare just getting to and from their hotel, much less a crime scene on an isolated waterway.

Bella swore to herself in the moment as she nodded over to a grinning Aunt Natalie. "Haven't seen a place this remote since we went with my parents down to see Grandpa and Grandma down in the Atchafalaya Backwater Basin," she said.

Natalie smiled. "Now that was an adventure."

"Wasn't it?" She smiled, letting the happy memories run through her head. For a minute, she was just happy to spend time with her aunt—an illusion that was shattered when they arrived at the department.

"Hello agents, I'm Chief John Tagomori. Welcome to the island of Molokai." A copper skinned man of Asian and Hawaiian descent bowed politely to the team as he made his introduction. "We'll bring you to the Hotel Molokai to wash and rest up after your trip. I'll warn you ahead of time, it won't be as plush as the Sheraton, but it has hot water for your showers. You'll need it after we get back from the location sometime tomorrow. That travel too will depend on the washed-out roads."

Rachel nodded after shaking the chief's hand. "I'm ASAC Gentry, Chief Tagomori. Thank you for reaching out and your assistance to the FBI." Then Rachel went to introduce the team to the chief. "This is Agent—"

Chief Tagomori pointed to a rolling thunderstorm headed their way. Bella could already feel the chill of rain in the air. "We can save the pleasantries for the office conference room later, ASAC. If we don't get a move on before that storm gets here, we'll be spending the rest of the early morning sleeping out in the jungle."

***Hotel Molokai***
***1300 Kamehameha V Highway***
***Kaunakakai, Hawaii***
***October 12th, 2023***

***5:45 A.M.***

Remote had been an understated word for Molokai. Primeval or ancient would have been a better description for the winding, mountain jungle roads. Bella had to catch her breath as she caught faint glimpses of jungle between blankets of towering fog. Onward, between the flashes of purple lightning from the storm, she caught a peek of the green and black mountains' silhouettes. She saw endless jungles cast in shadow, and the occasional shimmer of a winding stream. But everywhere they drove was darkness. As Bella continued to look out her passenger window wide-eyed and amazed, she was having trouble comprehending how any investigation—especially a murder investigation—could be conducted with any degree of accuracy in such hostile lands.

For most of the trip Chief Tagomori stayed quiet and reserved. But with the rain falling in torrents, he spoke calmly. "It's going to be a little rougher than I thought, agents. The storms have flooded a few of my backup roads. We'll have to chance the main stretch or—"

"Spend the day napping in the jungle. I caught that at the airport." George interrupted with a groan. Ever since his and Bella's lava tube adventure on the War Gods Case, George had grown a disdain for any jungle campouts.

Nodding to George and everyone, Chief Tagomori took his time. He had to, with the treacherous slide outs and tire spins caused by the deluge of tropical rain. Onward they trudged in the chief's off road vehicle, passing not one, but several flooded roads on their journey to their hotel in the town of Kaunakakai. The team drove from the eastern side of the island to the southern middle of the island into the largest town on Molokai, praying throughout to not get stranded along the way.

By sometime after five, with the graying light of day trying to breach the massive mountain fog, they pulled up to the haphazard and less-than-glamorous Hotel Molokai. After such an exhausting journey, Bella could care less what the place looked like. She needed a hot shower and a bed to rest her weary head.

***Molokai Police Department***
***74-88 Ainoa St***
***Kaunakakai, Hawaii***
***14:00 P.M.***

Molokai Deputy Chief Sampson Maeda arrived to pick up the refreshed FBI team at two o'clock. As Bella climbed into the rear passenger side of the Molokai off road vehicle, she caught her first sunlit view of the island. The afternoon sun had blazed back a large portion of the rain-induced fog, displaying the tallest mountains she'd seen since moving to Hawaii. The coastal winds from the Pacific pushed back the rest of the mist into the upper climes of the Molokai mountains, allowing Bella to view the winding, grass-swept coast with more twisting streams and towering waterfalls.

*I'm supposed to conduct a murder investigation and isolate clues in all this water and pristine beauty. This case has already had a rocky start. Now, we'll be tackling terrain unlike anything we have dealt with before.*

Twenty minutes after their drive, the team were escorted into the Molokai police department and straight to the conference room for the case debriefing. A tired Chief Tagomori was waiting with filed reports for each of Bella's team. Bella glanced over to a half-grinning Rachel and nodded. "This guy should be working for us."

"I agree. He reminds me of another grizzled agent who wants to retire." Both Rachel and Bella looked at Keith who raised a brow and smirked.

Keith put his hands together and leaned forward. "The way you and Harris are running the Hawaiian FBI Field Office, I'll need to have the funeral home ship my retirement packet to get my pension. Over forty years—who's counting after twenty—I've sacrificed for the FBI's greater good. The time—"

"You'll never retire, Agent Benton. The FBI will have to force you to quit. You are the very definition of a lifer." Rachel raised a half smile at him knowingly. "Besides, we need you now more than ever with these crazy cases."

"At some point kiddo, you'll have to fly solo on these things, Agent Gentry. Like we all do when the veterans head for the hills to live their final days." Keith shrugged and took a seat near the projector. Everyone followed suit.

The meeting began with Chief Tagomori having formal introductions of Bella's team. Then he introduced his officers in return. "We are at your full disposal and assistance. And, may I add, we are humbly honored to have Agents Natalie Roberts and Bella Walker on Molokai to help us."

Bella and Natalie both smiled politely. It wasn't lost on the others that the resemblance was uncanny.

Chief Tagomori nodded for the lights to be turned off and pointed to pictures of the crime scene. "Good morning. We recovered the body of sixty-year-old Roger Cheney three miles up Honouliwai Stream.

Best estimates on how long he's been floating in the water have it at four weeks."

A young officer in the back added, "I can't believe there was anything left, sir. That place is notorious for armies of coconut crabs." Bella shuddered remembering her last run in with coconut crabs and a body on the northwestern shores of Oahu.

The chief nodded to the next pic. It was a thousand or more crabs moving toward the floating man in the stream. To Bella, the picture looked like something conjured out of a nightmare. "Yes, it was a close call, Officer Pelletier. We beat the crabs' run this time." She glanced at Keith shifting uneasily as he watched the video of the crabs pinching out toward the officers.

Keith whispered, "I'm glad we get to watch the video and not have to retrieve the body this time." Everyone nodded but Victor. He was lost in contemplation, studying how the crabs meticulously swarmed and surrounded their prey. Bella shuddered again, wondering what the mad scientist might be thinking.

The Molokai chief continued as he waved for the slide of Cheney's wedding. "As best we can tell from witnesses, he was a defense contractor for Yellowrock on his honeymoon. The bride has skipped town before anyone could interview her. It's tragic that she won't be at her new husband's funeral. And it is truly unfortunate—due to the high rate of his body's decomposition—that we may never know what killed him."

Without missing a beat, Victor raised his voice to the ire of Natalie and the team. "Maybe I can help, Chief Tagomori."

"Agent Shelley, what the heck are you doing?" Natalie glared at him as Rachel pointed a warning to hush.

Agent Shelley stood with his hands out imploring. He opened his backpack to show the Ghost-in-the-Machine and pleaded. "I'll use the machine and no one else. What do we have to lose?"

Confused, Chief Tagomori furrowed his brow and crossed his arms. "What's he talking about, SAC Gentry?"

***Molokai General Hospital***
***Morgue***
***280 Home Olu Place***
***Kaunakakai, Hawaii***
***17:00 P.M.***

Victor shrugged and put his head down demurely waiting for Rachel's response. Assistant Gentry looked over to everyone shaking her head.

"Against my better judgment, you get to use your toy, Agent Shelley. But if I see the first sign of trouble, I'm pulling the plug. Are we clear?"

"Crystal, ma'am." Victor nodded and looked over to Chief Tagomori who was still perplexed. "I'll need to use your hospital's morgue, Chief. Where's the medical examiner's office?"

"That would be this way, sir. Why do you need to see Dr. Michener? We have given you everything from his reports." Chief Tagomori cocked his head and narrowed his eyes skeptically at Agent Shelley.

Agent Shelley narrowed his own eyes in indignant disbelief. "Why, I have to get him to sign a waiver for experimentation… on Roger Cheney's body." Chief Tagomori went wide-eyed and pale.

Despite the theatrics leading up to the second field use of the Ghost-in-the-Machine, Victor's machine was unable to repeat the results of its first outing. Roger Cheney had been too dead and way too decomposed to attempt a neurological link, and his past was too shrouded in mystery for them to put together a comprehensive data file for the machine to run through reconstruction scenarios. Unphased by what had occurred but disappointed, Agent Shelley rubbed his chin thinking.

"You did your best, Agent Shelley. It was a long shot." Bella tried to console the frustrated scientist as the Molokai police department ribbed him pretty good for its failure.

"What's the next plan, Agent Walker?" Rachel seemed ready to move on. Bella could tell her friend was uneasy about the Ghost-in-the-Machine and its quirky inventor. "Frankenstein here was a bust." Bella watched Victor wince at her verbal jab.

Bella didn't miss a beat as they drove with Chief Tagomori to the Molokai medical examiner's office. "First we'll go over the pathology follow up with Dr. Michener. I'm curious about his interpretation of what he saw in the toxicology reports. But my major focus is on his catalog of the intestine and stomach contents. If we find castor seeds—"

Rachel interrupted as her stomach groaned. "Agent Walker, I think I want to barf after hearing you say that. Couldn't you have waited to tell me that after lunch?" Bella's boss rolled her eyes as the team chuckled.

***Hotel Molokai***
***1300 Kamehameha V Highway***
***Kaunakakai, Hawaii***
***October 12th, 2023***
***19:00 P.M.***

Back at the hotel, Bella was left a note by Rachel to meet the team down at the beach for an impromptu dinner at Hiro's Ohana Grill. By the smiles and empty plates, Bella figured the food had to be excellent. Ordering the ribeye medium well, Bella sipped a coconut flavored drink with a paper umbrella while updating Rachel and everyone. "The poison was similar to the ricin found in the Hawaiian physics nuts. But there's a catch."

"And what's that?" Rachel asked while she sipped her own drink.

"Well, no one on the Hawaiian Islands had heard of this plant. Which got me to call Dr. Wecht for help. It brought back not so fond memories to him, folks." Bella took another sip of her drink as she looked over to her aunt. "One he said he hadn't seen anything like in quite a long time. Well, since the Sure-Kill Case, Aunt Natalie."

Natalie raised both eyebrows. "Oh really?" Bella could tell there was something her aunt was still holding back on. They'd have to have a private conversation about whatever it was later. "What was the second thing Dr. Wecht told you? I'm all ears to know, dear."

"We were able to identify nerium oleander from the stomach contents. A sliver of the wood was in the meat." Bella's ribeye showed up as she continued. She started cutting a piece of the tendered peppered meat to eat. "The problem is, of course, that this could be from anywhere. Nerium oleander is so widely cultivated worldwide they don't even know where it originated."

Keith nodded. "Down in Texas—Galveston, specifically—they have a big ol' festival every year. It's all over the island. And much of the south and west besides."

Bella nodded. "I saw that there's estimated twenty-five million oleanders planted on roadsides and highways in California. Which means just about anyone—or everyone—could have access to it."

"Well, that narrows down our suspect pool," grumbled Billy.

"Well, there is something here. The poison and some other plants in the mix—a salad possibly—came from Myanmar."

"I've never heard of the Myanmar criminal outfits on the Hawaiian Islands, Agent Walker. Are you sure it's not someone who wants us to think the man was poisoned in Myanmar?" Everyone at the table stared in disbelief at Aunt Natalie. "By your faces, I'm guessing you fine Hawaiian FBI folks are about to prove me wrong."

Bella slapped her hands together and looked over to her aunt with a grimace. As she spoke, her healed gunshot shoulder seemed to itch and irritate her a bit. "Aunt Natalie, let me tell you about disgraced Myanmar

General Arkar Sai—also known as The Spider. I'll enlighten you on our tangle with him in our team's case The Jade Princess."

Bella recalled briefly the lurid details with Aunt Natalie on her last assignment. When Bella was done, Aunt Natalie lowered her head and studied her empty plate. Bella waited for her to say something.

She smiled sheepishly and never said a word. But continued to be all ears.

# CHAPTER NINE

WITH THE STARS SHIMMERING OVER A SPECTACULAR BEACHFRONT night, Bella went over the follow-up results and notes from the assignments of each of her team members. "Agent Namara, let's start with you. What did you find out with Bangladesh?"

"They don't use curry to kill people?" Susan gave a giggle snort that had everyone shake their heads. Then she apologized for her bad joke and horrible laugh. "I'm sorry, Agent Walker. It's been a long day. It was a combination of two powerful plants. They were devil's trumpet and yellow oleander mixed in a specific combination that caused the victim to literally hallucinate to death. The devil's trumpet also hits the heart something fierce and may have caused a heart attack."

"Wow, that's old school occult killing right there." Keith leaned forward and narrowed his gaze as everyone waited for him to say more. "I worked a lot of crazy cases in Haiti and New Orleans. That was part of the zombification powders they used. That's how the Tonton Macoute kept their gangs in line in Haiti for sure. They'd scare everyone saying they could steal their souls and make them a zombie. Same went for the

Marie Laveau crowd in New Orleans. Except the latter was to bring in the tourists… I hope." Keith gave Bella and the team a mischievous grin.

Aunt Natalie took a slow, tired breath, "So I'm gathering Candace Kincaid—or whoever this Sure-Kill might be—used oleander as her primary poison. She'd dose them with whatever hallucinogen she could find then give them the killing stroke. Let's hope they didn't suffer too much."

"I second that, Agent Roberts." Billy nodded to her solemnly.

Bella thanked Susan for her hard work. Then she turned to Billy. "Agent Makani, what did you find in the Myanmar cases?"

"Same thing, Agent Walker. It was a super plant cocktail of rhododendron burmanicum, white poppy, and nerium oleander that was guaranteed to send you flying… straight into a casket." Billy showed everyone pictures of the plants on his phone. "With all the upheaval in Myanmar, white poppy production has ramped up. That flower alone could have taken the victims out. Someone went out of their way to make sure they never had a chance to add the other poisons."

"Thanks, Agent Makani." Bella looked over to Keith who gave her his initial introduction. "With Thailand, Agent Walker you can take your pick of plants that can mess a person up. I recall the Thailand shakes debriefing I gave to some rookie FBI agents prior to us celebrating a major victory on a case. Someone who will remain nameless, decided to try the shake anyway."

Keith rolled his eyes toward George Dwyer who seemed to be nervously tapping and looking away guiltily up at the stars. "Anyway, we found him in his underwear running through the jungles two days later believing he was a baboon."

"Well, good thing you found them, Agent Benton." Aunt Natalie winked at George.

"And the main cocktails found in the victims there?" Bella was trying to keep the gang on track.

"Cerbera odallam, jatropha curcas, and dieffenbachia maculate were the big three I found. I noticed one of these overlapped with the killings in Hawaii—jatropha curcas or the physic nut." Keith scratched his silver hair and rubbed his chin. "This killer really believed in leaving nothing to chance, I tell you. The ricin just in the psychic nuts was enough to murder a mule. Adding the other two just seemed like overkill. Pun intended folks." Bella gave a slight grin to the veteran agent.

"That it does, Agent Benton." George agreed as he pushed back the strands of his pencil-thin mustache. Then he raised a tired brow toward

Bella and Rachel. "I felt the same way on my case reviews of over a thousand of these poisonings, Agent Walker."

Nodding, Bella leaned forward in her chair. "There were probably more, Agent Dwyer. What did you find?"

"Each of the cases had one or more of these in their gut as a hallucinogen chaser—papver somniferum, mandragora, and nymphaea." George put his hands together as if to pray then spread out his fingers as he continued. "Then I spotted the real killers—atropa belladonna, hemlock, and henbane. I'll add that mandragora or mandrake was consistent throughout the poisonings, which isn't all that curious. That powerful plant can act as both a hallucinogen and an effective poison."

"Why do I keep getting the feeling we're up against a coven and not a serial killer?" Keith sighed and rubbed his temples. "Well, at least it's a start. Even if we have to cuff the Wicked Witch of the West in the end."

"We can't cuff her, Agent Benton." George gave his friend a broad smile.

"And why's that, Agent Dwyer?" Keith scowled as he went on. "Let me guess she has diplomatic immunity too like that accursed Spider."

"Nope. Dorothy threw that pail of water on her." Then in a cackling nasally voice that was an awful imitation of the *Wizard of Oz* witch. "Remember 'I'm melting! I'm melting!'"

The table erupted in an uproar of laughter. Not so much at what George said, but the god-awful way he delivered it. Even the scowling Keith had tears falling from his own belly laughs.

"While we are on the subject of magic, Agent Shelley, I have a question about the Ghost-in-the-Machine?" Bella heard the laughter from the table quiet down as her team looked on Bella with concern.

"Agent Walker, it was established we'd not be journeying back into that realm of the dead anytime soon." Victor took a sip of an iced tea and gave a side glance. "Harris as much as warned me that I'd be fired at a minimum."

Bella furrowed her brow and took a sip of her coconut and pineapple drink. Then she pursed her lips. "That's not what I'm asking. I want to know if you kept recordings of each of the machine's simulations. Seems like an obvious question and answer, sir. Were you able to record any of my own thoughts and images inside Candace Kincaid's mind? There must have been thousands of scenarios with each time she was murdered. Maybe we missed something with all the moving parts."

Agent Shelley rubbed his tired eyes and yawned before answering. Sitting up and looking at Bella, he seemed puzzled for a moment. "Yes, there were recordings. But they come across as brief snippets of irrational thoughts. It's hard to put them together into any form of linear progression. My guess—just like time and everything else—experiences, moments, and emotions aren't linear and as straightforward as we'd like. And maybe it should be that way. Quantifying or controlling free will isn't why I created this device. It's one of the reasons I lose sleep over the use of the device. I'm sometimes conflicted on whether the machine being introduced into the dead mind isn't just projecting rather than recording the actual thoughts. As with any experiment—no matter how planned out to mitigate gaps—uncertainty is always an inherent risk."

Rachel leaned back and crossed her arms. She looked at Bella for a minute then looked back at Victor with a raised brow. "So, give us your insight on what you discerned from thousands of memory snippets then. With that many random test samples to work with, we are dying to know your conclusions."

"Well, if you must know, I'll tell you." Victor stood a moment and walked out to the edge of the restaurant's deck overlooking the ragged sea cliffs. Then he turned back from the star-gemmed darkness and the roaring coastline. "Candace was specific in her kills. She planned out and timed each target's death. She never called them victims in any of the brief memory flashes. Each *elimination*—her words not mine—was a middle-aged man involved with defense contracts. And of course, by the simple pattern of the deaths, we knew that. But the introduction of data from Agent Walker's experience opened up several doors for us. She felt..."

"She was precise. Exacting," Bella jumped in.

"That's it," Victor said.

"Now some of the feelings I had make sense, Agent Shelley." Bella sighed as she explained. "I felt Candace's need to stick to details and regimen. She was removed. Unemotional to the end, despite her line of work. But she wasn't completely psychopathic. My heart fluttered, feeling her fears that she or her team might get caught. But the key moments to our case—her outrage, helplessness, and fear that her own kill team was hunting her—she told me. Her greatest terror was the uncertainty of all of it. As she ran for her life, I felt the terror of a betrayed asset for some organization with vast resources and reach. Like her targets—middle aged businessmen with defense contracts—her employer decided it was time to wrap up the final loose end."

Keith leaned back and took a drink of iced water. Resting his hands interlocked on his belly, "Well that's obvious from the poisonings across the globe, Agent Walker. We didn't need to climb into a dead assassin's skull to learn that—projected or otherwise."

"I agree, Agent Benton. Conventional investigative techniques have proved once again invaluable." Bella half smiled and saw Victor bristle. But then she brought up glaring mistakes by the alleged killer that were troubling. "But I'm bothered by what I saw in her head. For one thing, she didn't kill Alton Lincoln as ordered. Then, either she got majorly sloppy—not likely—or she wanted to be caught. That was evident when she didn't give her last target her trademark hallucinogens in the killing cocktail. Worse for her, Candace killed Alton in broad daylight in front of people. And the most unforgivable sin by Candace that surely got her killed—she stuck around on the crime scene."

Pushing back his raven hair and locking his hands behind his head, Billy added, "But Candace did kill him. And she gave that super creepy smile that she had done so, Agent Walker."

"Exactly, Agent Makani. She carried out the murder as ordered. She was this outfit's most proficient, expert killer. Usually, an assassin with that kind of track record, gets rewarded despite their screw-up. They get to live out their days in exile in some remote plantation villa or island retreat alone. But, in this instance, where I imagine staying in the shadows was a priority for a career killer, Candace failed miserably. However, even then, they retire a highly valuable asset like this or put them training new recruits." Bella took a breath and groaned in frustration. "Why did Candace's employer feel it necessary to eliminate her with her own kill team?"

"And the bigger question," chimed Natalie. "How many more Sure-Kill operatives out there?"

# CHAPTER TEN

***Hotel Molokai***
***1300 Kamehameha V Highway***
***Kaunakakai, Hawaii***
***October 13th, 2023***
***07:00 A.M.***

BELLA AWOKE THE NEXT MORNING WITH THE SOUND OF THE TURbulent seas roaring from out her front window. As she opened her eyes to the brilliant golden sunshine, she heard the ocean breeze shifting the palms just outside her window. Stretching and yawning, she decided to go for a morning run down a coastal trail before starting her follow-up with Dr. Wecht.

She put on her jogging pants and t-shirt and slipped her pale-as-a-ghost feet into her favorite comfortable cotton socks. Finally, she slipped on her gel running shoes, tied the laces at the door, and headed out for an epic run. It would clear her head and inspire her to a big breakthrough in this case. She was sure of it.

In the first five minutes of her jog, Molokai overwhelmed her.

Molokai's towering mountains loomed over Bella like shadowed giants ready to stomp. On she ran, past dense jungle forest and winding muddy roads. During the run she caught the powerful scents of flowers such as the pua and pikake, then recalled with a haunting chill the scents of the plumeria. The same flowers she watched falling in Candace's memories. It was in the last stretch of her run that a wave of drenching fog rolled down from a nearby mountain enveloping her. Between the sudden blanket of white and the growing jungle heat from the sun's further rise, Bella slowed to take a break. Inhaling and exhaling the saturated air that soaked and chilled Bella to her very core, she took a moment to look out on the horizon of the golden sun peeking out over the clouds.

*I've never seen a place as far removed from civilization. Well, except the further reaches of Timor Leste maybe. It's like I'm living on another planet rather than a Hawaiian Island.*

An hour later, long after her run and steaming hot shower, Bella dressed for work and reviewed Dr. Wecht's most recent analysis on Roger Cheney's death. The medical examiner on Molokai had overnighted newly obtained blood and tissue samples for further study by Dr. Wecht. It was a good call to get a follow up from the more sophisticated lab in Honolulu.

Looking at the first blood work and toxicology obtained, it was obvious there was little hope of discerning anything from the findings. Both the toxicology and labs from Molokai rendered nothing useful from the decayed man's body.

As if on cue, Bella's phone buzzed and she saw it was Dr. Wecht calling to follow up. "Agent Walker, we have been able to find something," he said excitedly. Not that it's conclusive with the amount of time Roger Cheney was decomposing in those warm waters. Before I deliver my findings, what was his background again? And by background I don't want what he did for a living. It's pretty obvious by now he had some affiliation with defense contracts. What I need to pin down is what country he was working out of?"

Bella took a sip of her coffee, burning her lips and almost dropping her cup. She'd forgotten to cool off the piping hot beverage after its brew in her room's coffee pot. Wiping her mouth and the counter she had placed the cup Bella answered. "From what Agent Makani dug up, he had a few lucrative contracts out of Myanmar. Laos, Cambodia. So, I'm guessing he was in Southeast Asia a lot following up on further bids."

Bella could hear the man sitting down. Then she caught the creak of his chair as if Dr. Wecht was leaning back. "That settles it. He was poisoned with a cocktail of plants from Laos. But there's an anomaly with this one, Agent Walker."

"What kind of anomaly? You just said it was the Laos cocktail that killed him." Bella took a sip of her bitter brew.

Dr Wecht hesitated a minute, sighing. Then, when he spoke, Bella couldn't believe what he had identified. "Oh, the plant combination certainly made Roger Cheney hallucinate and caused his heart to stop. But this sophisticated genetic delivery system that someone used to inject into his system is cutting-edge stuff. It's a strange, unnatural chimera, Agent Walker."

Bella rubbed her head and almost groaned in disgust. "Well, this confirms at least that the operators are on a professional level. Whoever Candace's employers are, they have access to some pretty sophisticated facilities."

"That's correct, Agent Walker. Not many labs in the world have access to this level of technology. It's a pretty hefty piece of research and development."

"Dr. Wecht, it goes without saying this was a big catch by you sir. So now we need to run all the old cases to see if this delivery system was used on the other victims, too. See if we can get any kind of bead on the method and trace it back to the source."

Dr. Wecht took a tired breath. To Bella the man sounded like he hadn't slept in a few days. "I thought as much, Agent Walker. That's why I called SAC Harris and advised him the minute I saw this marker in the victim. He authorized all the funding and personnel I can get over to Oahu to do just that. You'd be surprised how many lab techs don't turn down a free trip to Hawaii."

"I'm not surprised in the slightest Dr. Wecht. Thank you for all your assistance. This case is turning into the mess I thought it was." Bella hung up and stood with her coffee. Then she walked to the window and looked out to the vast sea.

***Hotel Molokai***
***Hiro's Ohana Grill***
***1300 Kamehameha V Highway***
***Kaunakakai, Hawaii***
***October 13th, 2023***
***11:00 A.M.***

With the sun still making its ascent across a cloud-filled sky, the FBI team had convened at Hiro's Ohana Grill for an early lunch before heading with the Molokai police out to Roger Cheney's kill site. Bella waited for everyone to sit and order before beginning.

Looking to Agent Dwyer first, Bella began. "George, what did you find out about our Mr. Cheney?"

Crossing his arms, George raised his right brow and leaned back. "Well, you would be surprised. I certainly was once I reached out to my contacts with the DoD. I got to see Roger at several high-profile defense contractor conventions. I saw one with him beside an alleged alien reverse-engineered spacecraft out of Roswell. That pic was kind of sketchy if you ask me." George shrugged and went on as his giant lobster meal was placed in front of him. Everyone's eyes went wide at the enormity of the seafood feast.

"Agent Dwyer, that lobster is as big as you. Where will you fit it all when you're done eating?" Agent Namara shook her head at the cooked crustacean and the man eating it.

"Focus back on the investigation folks." Rachel gave a slight growl to get the team to focus back to the case and away from George's cayenne-seasoned platter.

"Well, agents, the big kicker wasn't the alleged alien space vehicle at a defense contractor convention. The big news was the next couple of illicit photos of Roger Cheney with a beautiful, athletic woman with red hair and blue eyes." George lowered his gaze halfway to meet everyone's eyes before he took a forkful of his lobster.

Natalie took a sip of iced lemon water as the waiter placed a mahi-mahi poi bowl in front of her. Bella's stomach growled as her aunt took a bite of the lemon spiced fish mixed with the purple poi. "That's obvious it was Candace Kincaid." Then with a dismissive hand, "Or whatever her alias was for that assignment. What did you find out about her, Bella? I know you probably stayed up last night for hours trying to find something."

"You know me too well, Aunt Natalie." The waiter placed a rack of sizzling ribs in front of Bella topped with a pyramid of pineapple and barbecue sauce. Even George with a mouthful of his lobster stopped and stared at the dinosaur size rack of ribs.

Rachel, wide-eyed in disbelief that Bella would finish the meal, asked a caveman question to the laughter of all. "Did you steal Fred Flintstone's ribs, Agent Walker?"

Bella shrugged as she ripped off one of the pineapple-topped ribs. "No, Agent Gentry. But you may need to call him to finish this meal for me."

"So, Agent Walker, what about our dearly departed Candace?" Aunt Natalie had taken a second bite of her poi and mahi-mahi while asking.

"Liar, assassin, defense contractor, and world poisoner, Agent Roberts. She lied about her background to the police—which department and which murder take your pick. She was sighted, photographed, or identified by witnesses on several of the murders we have researched. But no one made the connection for some unknown reason." Bella took another rib and chewed a minute before adding. "Anyone that came too close to identifying and catching her were eliminated or pulled off the case."

"Are we sticking to the idea that this was one killer? Or several?" Billy asked as his heaping bacon spam burger arrived. "Certainly Candace wasn't the only one running this entire operation."

"I don't think this was *my* Sure-Kill," Natalie offered as she took a bite. "But the methods are the same."

"Then how can we be sure that this red-haired woman was Candace Kincaid at all?" Billy asked. "If she was in the company of Alton Lincoln for long enough to marry him, how could she have slipped out and been with Cheney?"

Bella nodded. "That's just the thing, Agent Makani. So either it was her—and she's already dead—or it was another assassin operating under her modus operandi. It wouldn't surprise me to find out that her employer has an entire team of Sure-Kill operators to carry out all their attacks. Which means we've got to climb the next rung of the ladder. Chasing down yet another assassin would be pointless. We've got to cut off the head of the snake."

"Which means finding commonalities for the targets. Was Dr. Wecht able to help us on the Roger Cheney death?" Rachel's meal had finally arrived. It was a salad topped with tropical fruits Bella had never seen before. One red thorny looking one in particular—lychee—Bella stared at in disbelief. "It's called lychee, Agent Walker. Would you like to try one?" Rachel offered one of her walnut sized red fruits to Bella.

"Thank you, Agent Gentry." Bella's mouth watered uncontrollably at the sudden surge of sweetness and tart from the fruit. "Wow, that caught me off guard. Tart and sweet like an apple and mango with a dash of sugar. Anyway, we have a team mobilized to assist the lab and Dr. Wecht is going to be putting in extra hours to help us."

Everyone seemed to look up from their meals surprised by the latest update. "Wow, he found something after all. To think Roger Cheney had been in the water for weeks. It's beyond incredible work by everyone, team. So, exactly what did he find anyway, Agent Walker?"

Eager with excitement at the tremendous find by Dr. Wecht and certainly a breakthrough in the case, "Dr Wecht identified a powerful and rapid poison delivery system." Bella presented the laptop with the presentation Dr. Wecht had forwarded. She pointed to the complex molecular structure. "This molecule is a chimera created in a lab somewhere using cutting-edge DNA sequencing. Then this lethal molecule is delivered into a specific target area of the cell using a sophisticated genetic transport system. The molecule can act to amplify the poison plant cocktail or act as a second poison to kill instantly."

Agent Shelley whistled in amazement. "It's pure genius. That's possibly the future holy grail of science."

Rachel gave him a sidelong look. "Another harebrained scheme of yours? Going to try to turn men into monsters?"

Victor shook his head. "Nothing of the sort. The potential for this sort of genetic—or metagenic delivery system— could be life-changing. It would make medications more consistent, more targeted. Less risk of side effects and more easily able to control the dosages. If whoever created this—whether it's Candace Kincaid herself or some organization she worked for—understood cellular biology this well, they could have easily cured cancer—may have actually, who knows." Victor stood and put his hands out angrily. "But instead of sharing the miracle of discovery and science to help the world, they chose to harm. To create a weapon out of a medicine. I know you may have some harsh opinions on my theories, but I never intended to harm anyone. I believe science is for the greater good of humanity."

"Sit back down, Agent Shelley. Your steak's getting cold," George cracked. Victor blinked, seemed to come back to his senses, and sat back down. But the team looked at him with a newfound sense of respect. For all his kookiness, it was obvious that Victor truly cared about humanity, which was far more than they could say about their killer—or killers.

"I'm sorry. It just… it burns me up that someone with the capacity to do wonderful things instead uses them to kill with such surgical precision."

"Like Jack the Ripper, Agent Shelley." Keith raised his head slightly with contempt. "Agent Walker, tell Dr. Wecht we are calling this thing the Jack the Ripper molecule for obvious reasons." Keith lamented with a groan then asked, "So is there an inoculation or Hell, an antidote to save a life? I know this killer or group doesn't plan on stopping. I'd like to be ready the next time we run across it."

# CHAPTER ELEVEN

***FBI Field Office***
***New FBI Morgue***
***Enterprise St***
***Kapolei, Hawaii***
***October 14th, 2023***
***10:00 A.M.***

THE TEAM FLEW BACK TO THE FBI FIELD OFFICE IN OAHU FOR A follow up debriefing with Rachel and SAC Harris. Once both had left, Bella, Aunt Natalie, and the rest of the team got to work figuring out who was Candace Kincaid—and what had placed her on the path of being a ruthless assassin?

"Every background check we tried to rustle up came up blank," grumbled Keith Benton. "No fingerprints, no DNA, no background, no Social Security, no nothin'."

"That isn't too surprising. Even accounting for all the fake names she gave investigators over the years, I can't imagine any of them were her true identity."

"Maybe she's like in Men in Black," Billy offered, which sent a round of groans through the room. "What? I'm serious. Maybe her employer went through and deleted her from every identifying database there was. Right on down to erasing her fingerprints."

Bella had to admit he had a point. "But who would have the capacity to do that, Agent Makani? To hack into federal databases, snap their fingers, and erase someone? It would take one hell of a hacker..."

"Or someone with massive resources," Keith finished. "If they can make a super-killer poison, if they can hire an expert assassin or team of assassins off the books, maybe they could do some computer hacking."

"It's looking more and more like Candace's employer has some pretty deep pockets," Natalie mused. "But where does it come from? What's their main source of revenue?"

"Their cover, you mean?" asked George.

She nodded. "Exactly. Where's the money funding all this—the high-tech bio research, the highly-skilled computer hackers, the international assassins? It adds up, and it has to come from somewhere. Operations like this rise when a major organization—a mega-corporation or a government, maybe a political party or a church or a bank or a mafia—wants to protect its interests."

George Dwyer whistled. "Are you saying our Candace Kincaid Lincoln was mobbed up?"

"Maybe not in the traditional way. But whatever she was involved in, it was certainly organized, and it was certainly a crime," Bella noted. "And if we can find a link to wherever she came from, we can find out more about whatever this organization is up to."

Natalie stood and walked over to view the rolling waves of the sea. Pausing a minute, she seemed to be drifting someplace else in her mind. "And that brings us back to the question we started with: who was she really, Agent Walker? What turned Candace Kincaid—or whatever her real name was, into this sadistic killer?"

"That's always the big question. Why did they do it?" Bella walked stood and walked over to her aunt. "Do you have any additional resources or contacts that might be able to help?"

Aunt Natalie gave a broad mischievous smile. "I know one sailor who is quite the expert in poisonings."

"Are you kidding me, Aunt Natalie?" Bella groaned as her aunt shrugged and raised her hands apologetically.

***The Salty Pirate Book Store***
***Nimitz Street***
***Oahu, Hawaii***
***15:30 P.M.***

Rachel parked the FBI cruiser with the team in the Nimitz Street parking lot across from The Salty Pirate Book Store. The traffic—never slow even on a weekday—was hustling and bustling as ever with locals and tourists alike. As the crosswalk signal lit to go, Natalie and Bella hastily crossed with Billy, Keith, George, Susan, and Rachel in tow. To Bella it seemed more agents than usual wanted to tag along. She guessed they were curious about the reunion of Natalie with Algernon.

Natalie was the most anxious as they dodged through pedestrians to their location. She practically broke into a sprint to reach the doors of the bookstore, and Bella had to scamper just at her heels behind. Bella smiled at Aunt Natalie as they went in. Bella couldn't help but feel the ever-present nostalgic charm of her first visit and encounter with the enigmatic and charismatic store owner: Algernon Magnum. Of course, Jimmy Buffet was still strumming along about being the son of a sailor as she opened the bat-wing wooden doors into the place.

"Welcome aboard, me hearties!" squawked an animatronic rainbow parrot, causing Natalie to roll her eyes and scowl.

The team, who had been snickering in anticipation behind her, all frowned. They'd expected the veteran agent to be shocked out of her wits the same way they all had been when first seeing the crazy contraption.

"That man will never change. He's had that squawking parrot longer than he's had the sailboat.

They walked further inside looking for the proprietor of the rustic pirate establishment. Bella watched as her aunt's eyes widened and she put a hand to her smiling mouth several times. They looked at each of the intricate walls of The Salty Pirate adorned with pirate memorabilia: muskets, maps, ship models, swords, and of course, pirate hats. Embroidered purple chairs were arranged in several places for patrons to sit and read the incredible collection of literature. Beautiful oil paintings of several styles of pirate ships from the Golden Age of Piracy—galleons, brigantine, and sloops—pirate renderings in charcoal, carved wooden ships and murals all highlighted the walls and shelves of the bookstore.

With wide eyes and a giddiness in her voice, Bella practically stammered. "Aunt Natalie, I always feel like Long John Silver will come around the corner and whisk me off to Treasure Island."

Natalie smiled. "And that's the allure of the rogue, the vagabond, and the pirate, my dear. Like Algernon—"

"They are never dull." A squawking parrot-like voice moved from around a book section that was an exact replica of Pirate's Alley in New Orleans' French Quarter. The towering man, with eyes the color of the sea, and graying red hair and beard, moved panther-like from dusting an impressive wax recreation of the great actor Yul Brynner as Jean Lafitte. Bella's mouth fell open at the attention to detail of Algernon's latest addition to his Jean Lafitte collection.

"That they are not, Algernon." Bella nodded with a pirate's smile.

Scratching his beard and narrowing his eyes to the team, "So, I see you have brought the whole department. What gives, young lady?"

Bella had turned to point to Aunt Natalie. But she had disappeared from her right side. Bella assumed her aunt had a reason and shrugged. "A forensic expert, a legend with the FBI, said you might know a little something of rare poisons."

Algernon put his hands up and scoffed. "I'm a pirate bookstore owner and occasional sailor, Agent Walker. Do I look like an expert in poisons?"

Bella looked over to Rachel and everyone before answering. Furrowing her brow and crossing her arms, "Now there, Mr. Magnum… Professor Magnum… Captain Magnum, if there's one thing I know about you… looks are quite deceiving."

"You might be onto something there, miss. Your aunt—"

"Her aunt is here, Algae." Bella grinned like a Cheshire cat as Aunt Natalie interrupted their conversation. The legendary aunt of Bella Walker was sitting in one of the plush upholstered chairs next to Yul Brynner with a book on Myanmar in her hand.

Algernon's face went sheer white, then a deep red. His jaw fell, and rose, and fell again. He rubbed his eyes, then pinched himself, as if somehow he wasn't believing what he was seeing. Bella and the others laughed at this while Natalie gave him a sly look.

"Well?"

"Well, I… I—well, I… well… Arrr!"

That set off another round of hooting laughter. Bella had never seen the squawking pirate captain so speechless.

"It's lovely to see you too, Algernon. Would that it could be in more pleasant circumstances than this one."

"Seems mighty pleasant to me," he recovered, somewhat more smoothly than he had first been.

She gave him a look that was an eerie mirror of a look Bella gave to Justin regularly. "Now don't you try unloading that charm on me, mister.

I'm not here for any extracurricular activities. We're going to need that hard-as-a-coconut head of yours to solve this one."

Algernon gulped, but quickly smiled. "Well, if there's one thing I'm any good at, it's cracking open this old coconut. What you got for me?"

Natalie fixed him firmly. "You remember the old Sure-Kill case?"

"What?" Bella watched Algernon's brow grow with concern. The very name of the lethal agent made his knees shake. "Oh, no. I thought she was retired. Or someone finally did us a favor and punched that viper's ticket."

Rachel moved up and added, "They might have, Algernon. We aren't quite sure though."

"If anything, it might be a whole nest of vipers," Susan said helpfully—or not-so-helpfully.

Algernon squawked. "What the hell do you mean by that?"

"It means that Sure-Kill is dead. But we may have a copycat, or an apprentice, or maybe a good-old fashioned team of killers," Bella said. "We're thinking that whoever employed the original Sure-Kill might have an entire network of trained assassins out there using the same methods."

Algernon slumped into his seat, a dumbfounded expression on his face. "It all makes sense. No wonder you could never get a bead on her, Nat. There were more than one."

Bella nodded. "That's our current line of inquiry, anyway."

"It gets better, Algernon." Natalie pointed to Bella. "My dear fool of a niece, climbed into her dead skull."

He furrowed his leathered brow, puzzled by Natalie's words. "Natalie Roberts, have you been swigging the rum? Because I could have sworn you said your beautiful, beloved niece climbed into a dead woman's skull?"

With Bella red-faced and out of sorts from her aunt's chastising and Algernon's compliment, Rachel explained briefly Victor Shelley's Ghost-in-the-Machine and Bella's bad idea. She described vaguely the interface and Bella told some—not all—of her experience inside the machine.

When they were done, and Algernon was sitting speechless, Natalie nudged him to say something. "Well, what do you think of all of it?"

Algernon rested both his arms on the arms of his purple upholstered chair. He took a deep sigh, then leaned back crossing his arms. "I think I might need the rum after hearing all that. Young Bella, how in the heck did you think talking to a dead killer was a good idea? I mean I have an entire library of supernatural horror tales that warns against it. And if you don't believe me, just read all of Edgar Allan Poe's words. Though I highly suspect his journeys with ravens and the dead were probably real. Anyway, what I'm saying is you pay a heavy price for communicating with the spirit world."

"I promise you, Algernon, I will never go back there again. But, I will say this." Bella took a sigh as Algernon ushered her to go on with a gesturing hand. "The effects after I came out of the void were truly haunting."

"Now, what's this all have to do with me, anyhow? Now, I may have a repository of legends and tall tales, mythologies and mysteries, and good old island history, but I don't know how I figure into this tale at all."

Natalie grinned. "Well, I seem to recall that you've got quite a bit of knowledge about poisonings. But that's not what I'm here for. I'm here for what you've got in the back."

"Now how would you know about that?" he asked. But Natalie held up a key and dangled it in front of him and he relented.

"You never cease to amaze me, woman."

"And don't you forget it."

An hour later, the team was loaded up with ten dusty boxes, each containing the archive of notes and files that Natalie had stashed away here for years.

Bella couldn't hide her curiosity any longer. "How did you get all these back there without Algernon knowing about it?"

"I'd like to know myself," said the pirate. The secret archive behind the statue of Jean Lafitte had led to a small storage locker buried so deep that Algernon himself hadn't taken notice of the boxes inside it.

Natalie gave an enigmatic grin. "Oh, you know. I'm pretty good at what I do. And to quench everyone else's burning curiosity, yes—I made copies of my case files when I was taken off the Sure-Kill case. I knew that there was a chance they'd mysteriously wind up missing or worse—permanently in the custody of some incompetent agent. I had them placed where I knew they'd be safe on the off chance Sure-Kill came back … and it turns out, I was right."

"Well, we'd better get back," Rachel reminded everyone with a tired smile. Then she nodded over to Natalie and waved for Bella to go. "We'll sift through these and see you later, Agent Roberts. I'm sure you have more of the case to discuss with this old salty dog."

Bella narrowed her eyes and gave a knowing half-smile before turning to leave. "Yes, I think she does, Rachel. Agent Roberts, make sure you pick his brain for sure."

For just an instant Bella glanced back to her mentor and her charismatic pirate. There was a seductive allure watching Natalie blush as

Algernon whispered something in her ear. Bella couldn't help feeling a warmth of happiness for the lost lovers reconnecting.

Outside, back in the world of traffic horns and tourist congestion, Bella twisted and dodged to catch up with her team. Taking in a breath after almost jogging to reach them, Bella slowed her pace in stride with the team before crossing the street as a cohesive group.

Billy Makani had a mischievous grin from ear to ear. "So, you know I have to ask."

Bella gave a stern gaze to Billy as they entered the FBI cruiser to head back to the office. "Tread carefully, Agent Makani. That's my Aunt Natalie—an FBI legendary professional in an interview with a decorated veteran."

"I agree, Agent Walker. Both are still at the top of their game in my book." Billy locked his seatbelt and looked out his window as Rachel prepared to leave the Nimitz parking lot.

"Well, what's your question, Agent Makani?" Bella dreaded his answer but asked anyway.

George locked in his seat belt and added with a smirk while rubbing his hands together. "This ought to be good." Bella saw everyone waiting—including Rachel—in anticipation.

"I saw two people today madly in love." Billy looked toward her with the sincerest of looks. Bella thought in the moment that she never wanted to play poker against Billy Makani. "How cool is it going to feel knowing your uncle is a bona fide pirate?"

The whole car burst into bellows of laughter.

Bella growled defensively. "Can it, Agent Makani!" There were more howls of laughter at her order. In response, Bella mumbled words under her breath at Billy's jest that would've made a sailor blush.

Half an hour later, and in the conference room of the FBI field office, Rachel updated the team on an event. "Team, tomorrow will be Alton Lincoln's funeral. His will had requested that he be buried in Kauai alongside his wife. Naturally, the family objected to his murderer being anywhere near him."

"I don't blame the family there." Agent Namara pushed back a strand of her hair while looking down at the table. "Why are we being given the funeral update, Assistant Director Gentry?"

"Well, Agent Namara, we try to limit the FBI going to funerals unless it's absolutely necessary." Rachel clicked a text with everyone's flight information and ticket number. "Being at Alton Lincoln's funeral during an investigation into his murder is one of them. A suspect or person of interest might just show up as well."

Everyone nodded and begrudgingly grabbed their overnight bags to catch the flight back to Kauai.

Little did Bella know as she attended Alton Lincoln's funeral on Kauai the next day, the whole affair would be quite a lively one.

# CHAPTER TWELVE

***Alton Lincoln Funeral***
***Kauai Memorial Gardens & Funeral Home***
***4716 Maalo Road***
***Lihue, Hawaii***
***October 15th, 2023***
***12:00 P.M.***

BELLA GAZED OUT AT THE LINE OF PALMS, FEELING THE WARMTH OF the tropical breeze on her face as she and the team had left their Kauai hotel just after daybreak to attend the formal wake. Now, as the line of cars parked for Alton's funeral Bella had the surreal experience of having a little more than a cursory idea of who Alton Lincoln had been. In the briefest of moments, she recalled his living face by starlight, the torch light in his eyes, and the salty taste of his lips as the plumeria flowers fell.

Groaning, almost wincing, she thought, *that damn ghost machine!*

Sitting in the discrete rear seats of the funeral ceremony, the team looked on at the growing procession still entering to pay their respects.

It was a menagerie of colleagues, friends, and acquaintances saying final words to the murdered man before he was laid to rest. Each agent kept a careful watch on anyone who might stand out or could be a person of interest. So far though, the stake-out of the funeral had been a bust.

As Bella canvassed the areas near the immediate family, she studied the various colorful arrangements of flowers—stunning plumeria varieties of course—and again had a moment. She was thinking of the image that had stuck from her time in the Ghost-in-the-Machine. It had been a Candace Kincaid moment that she hadn't been able to process before now. It was Candace's final fury and raging angst for having to kill Alton.

Watching him spasm beneath the waters of the river, she had almost dived in. But the key word—almost—had been just that. She had not saved him. And the fact that she had succumbed to that feeling of unfathomable fear that her employer would kill her disgusted and broke her. In a way, Candace knew killing the love of her life had not only broken her—it put the final nail in her own coffin.

"That's kind of odd, Agent Walker." George nudged her to glance to the right of the funeral forty feet away from Bella and her team. The area was staged closer to the casket but equidistant to Bella. The seating held a large square of astroturf grass with three white backed chairs. As Bella looked, George whispered as he nodded, "What's wrong here?"

Bella picked up on what George was alluding to. A picturesque, towering, raven-haired woman with the physique of a gymnast strutted forward. She looked like something straight out of the Addams Family—and twice as deadly. She wore an expensive black dress—possibly Louis Vuitton—large black hat, and netted black veil to hide her porcelain face. Two enormous, linebacker-sized bodyguards were to either side of the woman. The men wore military-style high and tight crew cut hairstyles, dark sunshades, and were attired in black formal suits. And all three appeared to be carrying weapons… at a funeral!

Bella whispered back without letting her eyes drop on the woman and her guards. "Odd, indeed, Agent Dwyer. Everyone keep your eye on that trio and possibly others. We may be chatting with them shortly."

Everyone went silent as a priest—Father Gilbert Perez—walked solemnly to the podium next to the ebony casket of Alton Lincoln. He introduced himself to the growing crowd of onlookers. He began the eulogy with a fire and passion that Bella had never witnessed before at a ceremony for the dead. "Ladies and gentlemen, we are gathered here on this lovely day to see our heavenly brother, Alton Thomas Lincoln, off to a golden world beyond this one. That's right, he's headed into our

Heavenly Father's embrace. His journey was tragically cut too short. But his journey with the Lord shall last forever and ever."

Father Perez looked out to the crowd as the wind gusted slightly off the pine topped mountain behind him. Then seeing he had everyone's attention he began again as the wind died down. "Be comforted in this moment by the cherished words of David in Psalms 116.

*I love the Lord, for he heard my voice;*
*He heard my cry for mercy.*
*Because he turned his ear to me,*
*I will call on him as long as I live.*
*The cords of death entangled me,*
*the anguish of the grave came over me;*
*I was overcome by distress and sorrow.*
*Then I called on the name of the Lord:*
*"Lord, save me!"*

Bella heard a whizz and looked in the direction, confused. Then there was another. At first it didn't register what had happened. But only for a moment then she thought,

*A silencer! Someone is shooting at us!*

In that same moment, Bella was knocked to the ground by someone and protectively covered—Aunt Natalie.

"Everyone get down!" Natalie bellowed.

Twisting, she and Natalie scrambled for safety anywhere. In their erratic search to hide and return fire, Bella heard a woman scream in terror, possibly shot.

The scene erupted into chaos as the crowd dispersed, screaming and running for their lives. But Bella already knew the right place to look. She dove behind a chair for cover and turned—and sure enough, the strange woman in black and her two hulking bodyguards were advancing, their weapons drawn.

With the speed of a cat, she drew her weapon, checked it, raised it, and fired, hitting one of the huge men in the knee. Then as she provided cover fire for Billy and Keith, she caught the voice of Father Perez yelling for everyone to seek shelter. There was another whizz past her head and Bella hit the ground scrambling. In the instant it looked like the second bodyguard might shoot both men, Agent Namara had positioned herself behind the man and screamed, "Drop your weapon, now! On the ground!"

With a gun directly at his head, and Agent Namara with a kill shot, the behemoth protector of the strange lady in black dropped his gun and went to his knees. Bella moved in as Agent Namara kept cover and handcuffed the man. Their captured suspect had a gunshot to his arm but seemed unphased. Looking to her left, Bella saw George had already cuffed the other guy she had shot in the knee.

Turning to cuff the woman in black, Billy yelled out angrily, "Agent Walker, she got away!"

Bella barked out orders as she, George, and Susan moved one of the shooters. "She won't be far, Billy. Spread out and find—"

Bella was interrupted by the roar of a powerful engine and the squeal of rubber tires on asphalt. She watched in a helpless rage as a car raced away in the distance. Everyone heard the roar of that engine and watched as a red Dodge Demon 170 blasted away to escape in seconds. Billy darted after it as fast as he could, but before he could get close enough to catch the license plate, it had turned a corner and left him in its dust.

Bella cursed and kicked over a chair in frustration. Then she heard the laugh of the shot bodyguard and grimaced in anger knowing who was in that car.

"Good luck catching her, *Agent Walker*." The bodyguard with the shot arm smirked as Bella led him to a police squad car. She yanked him a little harder than was strictly necessary, but she didn't feel an ounce of guilt for it. Not after the man had just shot up a public place.

"We'll get the bullet out of your arm at the local hospital." Bella pointed to the blood saturating his bandage that had been placed by paramedics. "Then we'll talk. As it stands now, you're looking to do twenty-five to life at a maximum-security facility for firing on federal agents at a funeral. But—"

"I'm no rat." The shot man growled and flexed his handcuffed shoulders.

"Don't these guys all say that?" Bella rolled her eyes over to Keith already trying to get the suspect to cave. "Then the longer you sit in a cell, and the longer you think of the rest of your life behind bars, the more the idea of ratting out your handler or employer, becomes a great idea. We really want them… not you."

***Wilcox Hospital***
***3-3420 Kuhio Highway***
***Lihue, Hawaii***
***October 18th, 2023***
***15:00 P.M.***

Both bodyguards were transferred by EMS with police escorts to Wilcox Medical Center. Three days, two emergency surgeries later to both men, two lead FBI bullets removed from both, and resting comfortably, Bella and the team followed up with both in guarded rooms.

Twenty-four grueling hours of FBI interviews later, Sergeant Abraham Schwartz cracked under the enormity of a life behind bars. His colleague, Gunnery Sergeant Wolf Conrad, took twenty-five hours to cave but corroborated what his teammate had said.

"You're damn lucky nobody was killed, Sergeant, or we'd be a lot less inclined to hear your side of the story," growled Bella, with her arms crossed and a fierce glower on her face.

"Can I have anything for this pain? It burns like fire, Agent Walker! Ibuprofen and Tylenol ain't touching the fever either."

"You'll have to call the nurse for that." Bella made no move to press the call button, though.

With sweat pouring from the intense pain and fever caused by the bullet removed from his left knee, Gunnery Sergeant Conrad exclaimed desperately, "Like Schwartz said. We just got roped into this gig by our new employers. They were paying sweet for less risk—or so we thought. I swear, neither of us knew you were federal agents. They gave us fifty thousand dollars each, offered us a great lodge on the beach where we met Sure-Kill for the—"

"Hold on. Did you just say Sure-Kill?" Bella looked at Billy and then back to Gunnery Sergeant Conrad.

"Yeah, Sure-Kill. Why, do you know her?" Wincing in pain and begging for more medications, Wolf added as Bella rubbed her forehead. "Yeah, she just got moved up to the top dog position with Yellowrock after killing English Ivy."

Bella frowned. "Who the hell is English Ivy?"

# CHAPTER THIRTEEN

***Wilcox Hospital***
***3-3420 Kuhio Highway***
***Lihue, Hawaii***
***October 18th, 2023***
***20:00 P.M.***

KEITH AND SUSAN CONTINUED THE FINAL QUESTIONING WHILE Bella went grab a hot coffee processing what she had just heard from Gunnery Sergeant Conrad. Bella shook her head walking out in disgusted at what she had heard.

*They were just following orders from Yellowrock. If they can be believed. But how many militant despots have used that defense? Too many.*

At the coffee pot in the nearby medical breakroom, she blew heated mist off her brew pondering again on the words. George walked up and asked as he poured his own cup of coffee. "What do you think?"

"What I think is this is all a little too convenient, Agent Dwyer. They just show up and start blasting out of nowhere and then let themselves be caught? Why bother with all the expensive assassinations, the federal hacking, if you're going to just dangle it in front of our faces like that? It's like they think we're stupid."

"Well, maybe they're right to think that. For some of us, at least," he amended quickly, gesturing to himself.

Bella chuckled. "Don't sell yourself short, George. I know there's still something working in that brain of yours. Even if those cogs up there are a little rusty and full of cobwebs."

George took a sip of his black coffee and grinned. "You want to know what I think? I think they are cogs in a bigger wheel. They had their orders. I'm not surprised they didn't know hers. It's how these companies all operate. Plausible deniability is their bread and butter when they're outed."

Bella chuckled silently. "See? I knew there was something up there. Why, you just identified the problem with all our politicians with that insightful remark."

"Maybe I should retire too. I could have quite the future in politics," he said scornfully.

"You are always the comedian, Agent Dwyer." Bella shook her head and sat for a minute rubbing her tired head. "I couldn't take enough showers to wash off the corruption and filth these guys orchestrate. Much less, could I look at myself in the mirror each morning and not feel some sort of shame with the deals I'd have to make to be a politician. Too many compromises of your soul."

"Do you buy the protection angle? You know, all they know is they were assigned to protect Sure-Kill wherever they went." George sat across from Bella and leaned back in the flimsy hospital chair.

"Yes. You saw those two steroid-amped goons. Neither has the IQ of pond scum—no offense to the pond scum. They were hired muscle so she could kill a target and take the heat off her. Imagine their surprise when they came to a funeral and Sure-Kill tried to eliminate an FBI agent. It's probably the only reason any of us are still alive."

"How, so, Agent Walker?" George leaned forward and took another sip of his coffee.

"Well, you have to admit killing a federal agent at a funeral is bit much for any assassin. I think they had two motives here. First, somebody wanted this case shut down at any cost. Even if it meant exposing the outfit. Had they killed one of us ..."

"You mean you, Bella. It's obvious they wanted to take out the lead agent with the six bullet holes in your chair." Aunt Natalie walked in, sipping a bottled water, and took a seat.

Bella nodded and continued. "And second, while we were distracted with all this, they would have sent their agent to 'take care' of another target. Use the chaos of a mass shooting—and possibly murdering an FBI team—as cover to pull off a major operation. Throw these two knuckleheads to the wolves—who probably won't see trial by the way this gang operates—while Sure-Kill strikes another target. Hell, she may be working right now, and what are we doing? We're sitting in a hospital."

They sat there for a moment contemplating things. Bella knew it was a stretch on a stretch on a stretch, but she was following her gut.

"You think they really are Yellowrock?" George asked.

"I think if we press them on it, the company will deny and deny and deny. And something tells me there won't be much of a paper trail to follow up on. But Aunt Natalie saved my bacon, and we caught two of their guys. So not a total loss." Bella lowered her head and half-smiled. "Thanks, by the way, Aunt Natalie."

Red-faced, not realizing the weight of her heroics to save Bella, Natalie tried to downplay the moment. "You'd have done the same, dear niece. It's what we do, you know."

George readjusted his wobbly seat and said, in his typical sarcasm, "Well ladies, this butterflies-and-balloons happy moment is nauseatingly sweet. Now can we please get back to finding this assassin? Where the hell is that crazy woman Sure-Kill?"

Both Natalie and Bella rolled their eyes at him. Once again, it was like seeing double in their expression.

"You have such a way with words, Agent Dwyer," spoke the older woman. "Well, we know she's on this island or at least hope the island lockdown worked. But exactly where she is, I have no idea. Any suggestions of where, anyone?"

Bella pursed her lips and shrugged. She had an idea that might further shed light on the investigation. "Let's go talk to our good friend Sergeant Schwartz. George, maybe I'll show him that picture on my phone of Candace Kincaid."

"Sounds like a righteous plan, Agent Walker." George nodded as the group left the breakroom.

With an irate nurse following the team in tow, upset that they were waking her patient Sergeant Schwartz, Bella waved her off and entered the room. "Okay, Sergeant Schwartz, one more question and then you can rest up."

The freckled faced ginger-haired man gave a wolfish smile. Putting his arm up he gestured with an open hand. "Shoot, Agent Walker."

Bella showed him a picture of Candace Kincaid. Sergeant Schwartz shrugged as he stared at the picture for a second. "That's English Ivy. She was one of the top assets for the company until she got sloppy. Sure-Kill eliminated her."

"How did she get sloppy, if you don't mind me asking?" Agent Dwyer looked over to Bella then Sergeant Schwartz with a nod.

"That's simple enough, Agent. She broke the number one rule." Sergeant Schwartz took a deep breath and looked at his shot arm. "She fell in love with her target."

Keith and Susan were just outside Sergeant Schwartz's door. Keith ushered Bella to come out of the room. Bella turned just a moment back to the bodyguard. "Thank you, Sergeant Schwartz. We'll do our best to keep you and your partner safe."

"Good luck with that, Agent Walker." Sergeant Schwartz wiped a bead of sweat off his brow. "Yellowrock has a reach you can't even begin to fathom. I'm not a fool, Agent Walker. I know the score. We were dead the minute we screwed up and didn't kill you."

Optimistically, George raised a slight brow before he and Bella walked out of the room. "Well, there's a bright spot, Sergeant Schwartz. At least you came clean and cleared your soul."

"Yellowrock isn't responding to any comment or request for paperwork," Keith reported as the team walked out of the hospital. "Shocker there. I guess for all the defense subsidies they get, they don't seem too happy to talk to the FBI."

"Well, that part of the story at least bears out. And we now know English Ivy was the code name for Candace Kincaid." Bella paused outside of Wilcox Medical Center to look toward the sea. Then she turned to Keith. "But what's the business connection between Yellowrock, her, and Alton?"

"Easy enough." Susan passed along a folder containing five years of investment reporting with Yellowrock. The top donor at each of their events was—"

Bella's face tightened as she looked up from reading the reports. "Alton Lincoln."

"Bingo."

She kept reading. "He was a partner with Yellowrock. He wasn't just an employee but an investor. He was a headhunter spearheading new acquisitions. Basically, he went out and gathered all the clients for Yellowrock."

"Correct, Agent Walker." George looked to Keith and back to the rest of the team as they climbed into their rental car. "But, why in the world would you kill the guy bringing in all the money? Seems to me you promote a guy like that or buy him out."

"Jealousy, power, and greed are powerful things, George. Maybe the board figured they could share more profits without him." Bella frowned as she locked in her seatbelt.

"Yeah, those things happen way too often, I tell you." George sighed as he looked out his passenger window. "Now what?"

"We phone Rachel and SAC Harris. This particular part of the case just went well over our paygrades. We'll need their political expertise to navigate these treacherous political waters." Bella took her own sigh as the team drove to the hotel to pack for the flight home.

***FBI Field Office***
***Enterprise St***
***Kapolei, Hawaii***
***October 19th, 2023***
***09:00 A.M.***

"These low-down scumbags in Washington never cease to amaze me in their utter depravity!" Harris was pacing as Bella walked into his office. Rachel was sitting across from him sipping a green tea and shaking her head. She offered water to Bella from Harris's fridge.

"Yes, they have a penchant for nefarious behavior, sir." Bella nodded and sat in a chair next to Rachel.

"I demanded a meeting with Yellowrock's CEO Harry Finch and the Director of DARPA, John Taurus. I put out formal emails and sent attached letters." Harris sat and leaned in with hands interlocked as if he was praying.

"That's a great start, sir. And what did their legal teams say?" Rachel was trying to calm her boss. Bella could see her distractive tactics were having little effect.

Harris huffed. "We got assurances from both men's legal teams that they are cooperating with our investigation. We had promises that they would be here in my office by nine A.M."

Bella took a sip of her lemon water. "It's nine-thirty, sir. Maybe there was a delay at the airport."

"They both have private jets. The weather from Washington D.C. was perfect for flying. And there were no breakdowns, stalls, or anything to delay these men to be here on time. They're stalling for time, is the only stall I see."

"If I may, sir, why DARPA?" asked Bella.

"Why, Yellowrock just landed a huge partnership with them, of course. Don't you watch the news, Agent Walker?" Rachel's voice was teasing, but the tiredness in her face told a different story. It told of a long, sleepless night of research, phone calls all the way across the country, and paperwork nightmares.

"Experimental metagenic injections… all sorts of who-knows-what about poison methods… I have to say, it makes sense. Some of the stuff that comes out of that agency sounds like science fiction," Bella said.

"And considering your own recent excursion into the veil beyond, it seems that science isn't always so fictional anymore," Harris said.

Bella chuckled. "That's one way of putting it."

The hour crept past ten before Harris's administrative assistant knocked gently on the window. Harris ushered her in. "Sir, we've got an update."

With his eyes narrowed and a stern look, "Well, get on with it. Everyone on our side showed up for the meeting."

She smiled politely and looked down at her tablet. "The legal teams of both parties humbly apologize for their clients' inability to attend the meeting here in Hawaii. Pressing matters of a discrete nature prevented them from coming. However, in the spirit of interagency cooperation, DARPA will be sending their brightest professional to follow up—Assistant Director Rick Fern. And not to be outdone, Yellowrock will send their Chief Operating Officer Valerie Carrington."

Director Harris put his hands behind his head and leaned back in his chair. "That's just peachy. When can we expect these fine professionals?"

The young woman cleared her throat. "Well, sir. They should be here in two days."

Harris groaned in seething disgust.

# CHAPTER FOURTEEN

***FBI Field Office***
***Enterprise St***
***Kapolei, Hawaii***
***October 21st, 2023***
***9:00 A.M.***

TWO DAYS FROM THE ORIGINAL REQUESTED MEETING, DARPA Assistant Director Rick Fern remained a no-show. There was no follow-up explanation from the agency nor was anyone taking SAC Harris's calls. His temper was again at full boil.

But one minute before the scheduled meeting, a tall, striking brunette strode confidently into the office. She didn't even so much as break her stride as the onlookers began murmuring and whispering—only removing her stylish designer sunglasses as she entered the lobby. They were quickly and efficiently placed into a Salvatore Ferragamo bag slung over her left wrist as her heels clacked on the tile floor. It went without saying that she was Yellowrock COO Valerie Carrington.

She kept her face perfectly still as she approached the security office and the uniformed guard gave her a cursory pat down.

"Your phone, ma'am," said the guard, holding out her hand for it.

"You can't be serious."

"No outside phones in the building."

Valerie reached into her bag and produced the phone, where it was taken by the guard and placed into a locked deposit box. The guard handed her a key.

"You can pick it up on your exit. Have a nice..."

The guard trailed off as she snatched it and stormed off quickly. Some of the more immature men in the office began openly gawking, at which Rachel rolled her eyes as she and Bella escorted the woman to the conference room.

"Nice of you to join us. I'm ASAC Rachel Gentry."

"The pleasure's mine," Valerie replied automatically in a clipped monotone. There was no warmth, or indeed, pleasure, in it.

Bella traded a silent look with Rachel as they made their way back. Somehow, they had to make this woman crack—but right now, she was looking like a robot. She idly wondered if Valerie Carrington was yet another product of whatever mad science this organization was up to. Had they found a way to erase the emotions and feelings of their operatives—and replace them with cold calculations?

She shook the thought out of her head. She was starting to tread into conspiracy territory now. What she needed were facts.

With his eyes locked intensely on the nervous executive, SAC Harris set the benchmark on how the meeting would play out. "It goes without saying Ms. Carrington, that you are late—two days late—by my reckoning. If this misdirection and lying continues from Yellowrock, we can go ahead and skip the formalities and serve arrest warrants right now."

"My apologies, SAC Harris." She took a seat. "We intend to fully cooperate with the FBI. Mr. Finch was busy with—"

"Pressing matters, yes, yes. I'm sure. Well, let's get the formal introductions over with, shall we? You've already met Assistant Special Agent in Charge Rachel Gentry and Special Agent Bella Walker. To her left is Agent Natalie Roberts." Harris went through the rest of the team who greeted Valerie. That would be the last of the congenial pleasantries for the rest of the interview.

"Now, you've been apprised of the questions we have for you?"

Valerie gave a short, imperceptible nod. Her steely blue eyes remained impassive and unimpressed as she stared down the assembled

FBI team. It was beginning to feel like a standoff, and they hadn't even begun.

Harris slid the photos of Schwartz and Conrad across the table to her. "We've arrested two of your employees as perpetrators of a mass shooting—an attack on federal agents, I might add."

"I've never seen these men in my life," the woman replied curtly. "They're not in Yellowrock's employ."

Harris lowered his head so the light coming in from the window glinted off his glasses. He'd been expecting this, of course. "Well, they claim they are, Ms. Carrington."

"I'm sure they'll claim whatever they can to save their own skins."

"Even a claim that Yellowrock ordered the assassination of multiple federal agents?"

She gave Harris a steely glare. At that moment, Bella thought it was not unlike the hardened gaze of Candace Kincaid. "As I said, Mr. Harris, these men can claim whatever they like. But you can't seriously expect us to fly out to Hawaii to respond to every whispered conspiracy or slanderous claim, can you? I'm here as a courtesy to you, but that's all this is. A courtesy."

Bella bit back the scathing reply she'd have liked to say, and a quick glance at Rachel and Natalie showed that they too were chomping at the bit to fire back at the woman. But they held back, allowing Harris to run the show.

"So Yellowrock wouldn't mind providing the Bureau with employment records confirming that Mr. Schwartz and Mr. Conrad are, in fact, not connected to Yellowrock in any way?"

Valerie rolled her eyes openly, the first display of emotion she'd given all morning. "And the Bureau wouldn't mind providing a warrant for that information?"

Harris grumbled. "We hope that in the interest of cooperation, and national security you could provide this information."

The woman snorted. "National security? You must be joking? What the hell does the Bureau have to do with national security?"

Rachel had had enough. "Ms. Carrington, if you don't cooperate with this inquiry, we'll—"

Valerie silenced her with a withering gaze. "You'll what? Charge me with obstruction? You're welcome to try. But as it stands right now, you have no charges. No proof. No evidence, no facts, nothing but the half-cocked theories of a couple of crazed shooters trying to save their own skins." She turned back to Harris and tilted her head. "As for the employee records, those actually *are* a matter of national security."

Bella narrowed her eyes, ready to launch her own salvo, but the hand of her aunt stopped her. Natalie leaned over and whispered into Bella's ear. "Keep an eye on her body language. She's getting tense. More dramatic. We're getting closer."

Bella responded with a questioning look before Natalie clarified, "Wait for an opportunity."

She didn't want to nod, to give anything away, but she didn't need to. The look she gave her aunt communicated everything.

"...that's classified information," Valerie was saying when Bella returned her attention to the proceedings. "I understand that you have a procedure to follow, but my employers handle highly sensitive information on behalf of the Department of Defense. We cannot divulge any of this without the proper vetting and security clearances. In the interest of national security, of course."

"Right," Harris growled. He was obviously getting frustrated. Rachel took note of this and jumped in—much more diplomatically this time.

"Ms. Carrington, can you think of a reason these two men have claimed that they—and a team of assassins—are on Yellowrock's payroll? Much of the publicly available information we have discovered doesn't seem to indicate that Yellowrock is in the field of murder."

"We are in the defense business, Agent Gentry. We only provide operational resources—tanks, planes, technology, personnel, and state-of-the-art unmanned aerial projects. Our operations and clients are sensitive, and—of course—classified."

There it was. Her opening. Bella leaned forward. "Would that include genetic research?"

Valerie cleared her throat. "As I said before, I am just the nuts and bolts of Yellowrock. The day-to-day operations person who keeps the lights on. But I can assure you, every one of our projects and divisions is fully in compliance with DARPA and DoD guidelines."

"We have... sorry, one moment," Bella said. She flipped quickly through her files to pull up the list of labs capable of pulling off the high-tech genetic research to create the poison delivery system. She had poured over it for hours and hours in the last two days, highlighting and marking possible connections to known Yellowrock facilities—including a few that seemed too coincidental to be true.

She turned the folder around and slid the list across to Valerie. "Can you confirm the contents of the list and these addresses?"

The woman gave her an apprehensive look before reviewing the document quickly. "It seems these are Yellowrock facilities," she said. "This is all public information."

"Take a look at line thirty-seven for me, if you don't mind. I had a particular question about this facility. What do they do?" She tapped the highlighted line.

"Research and Development Studio 17, in San Diego," Valerie read off. "As I've previously mentioned, the information is—"

"Classified, of course," Bella said. "But the thing that caught my eye is the real estate history of this particular facility. It seems that Yellowrock acquired this in a bulk purchase along with several other facilities—you'll see the others highlighted on lines fourteen, nineteen, twenty-six, and fifty-three—as part of the acquisition of Marble Digital Solutions a few years back."

"I'm aware."

"Now, see, we have to dig a little deeper. You see, all the other facilities purchased from this sale seemed to fit Yellowrock's model. Software production, manufacturing, IT labs, that sort of thing. But this lab in San Diego was a little unusual. This particular facility was operated and run by one of Marble's subsidiaries: the Pacific Metagenics Institute, or PMI."

Valerie sighed. "Can you please get to the point, Agent?"

Bella held up her hand. "I'm working on it. You know, all these generic names you defense contractor types choose really makes it tough to dig up some of your details. But not impossible. So, I poked around a little at what PMI did, and wouldn't you know it? Back in the late nineties and early aughts they came under investigation briefly for the development of experimental genetic altering and the development of highly dangerous substances. The stated claim, of course, was that it was for the development of new and more efficient medicines, anesthesia, painkillers, those sorts of things. But the facility's director at the time was quietly dismissed and much of it was all covered up. Of course, he was given a pretty hefty golden parachute as well. The disciplinary and court proceedings are, of course, sealed, but I was able to look into some additional information..."

It was Natalie's turn to take the baton now, and she produced a file of her own—one of those that had come from the buried treasure in Algernon Magnum's shop.

"It's the most curious thing, Ms. Carrington," Natalie started. "This information has been completely wiped from every FBI database available. It's a good thing I made hard copies when I worked this case back in the day. And I found a wealth of information about the lab and facilities down there in R&D number 17 in San Diego. Including, most particularly, the development of an injection method with direct correlation to the recent kills of the assassins known as Sure-Kill, English Ivy, and... well, who knows how many more are out there."

Valerie's eyes flashed briefly at the mention of the name Sure-Kill, but she betrayed nothing more. It was time for the piece de resistance.

"Oh, and that director of PMI? His name was Roger Cheney," Bella said. "He resigned from PMI to avoid charges, and wouldn't you know it, he jumped ship straight to Yellowrock, where he was placed in charge of 'Emerging Technology Research'—code, I'm sure, for everything from biological weapons to artificial intelligence research. And it was at *his* direction that Yellowrock purchased Marble Digital, just to get that PMI lab back."

The steely-eyed executive pressed her tips into a tight line.

"You know what I think?" asked Rachel. "I think that Mr. Cheney here had a sudden crisis of conscience, who knows what or why, and wanted to come forward to the FBI about it. And I think ever since the beginning, you had an operative watching him—this gorgeous redhead right here," she said, pointing to the photo of the two of them twisting in bed, "and ready to pull the plug if he threatened to reveal Yellowrock's secrets."

Valerie Carrington pushed away from the table and stood up. "I don't have to listen to this anymore. This is nothing but pure speculation. You're fishing, agents. If you're going to waste any more of my time, come back with charges."

"We have just one more thing, Ms. Carrington," Harris said as she turned to leave.

"What?"

"Were you aware that the FBI raid on that facility in San Diego turned up evidence of continued genetic testing with dangerous, banned substances? A new program started under the direct orders of CEO Harry Finch?"

Her eyes went wide, and she stiffened. She recovered after a minute, but the damage was done. "I—I wasn't aware there was an FBI raid on that facility," she finally stammered.

Harris chuckled, almost pretending like it had been a faux pas to mention it. "Oh, of course. It was carried out early this morning. The team locked down all external communications so your corporate office wouldn't have heard of it just yet. The press conference isn't for another couple hours, where I'm sure you'll find out all about it."

"I'll... I'll see myself out."

"It was a pleasure meeting with you, Ms. Carrington," Harris called after her as she hurried down the hall.

"Don't forget your phone!" Rachel added.

The second she left the room, everyone exhaled a sigh of relief and a round of high-fives went around.

"Excellent work, team. We've got them on their back foot," said Harris. "It's obvious Finch made her the fall guy for the company while he made his getaway. Now we just need to get a bead on Mr. Finch himself."

"How are we going to do that, sir?" asked one of the agents that had been waiting in the back.

As if to answer, Harris's phone beeped. He held it up to his ear and couldn't help a broad grin from crossing his face. "Very good. And you got it planted? Of course. Give the team down there my thanks."

He hung up and announced to the team waiting with bated breath. "It seems our good friend Ms. Carrington will lead us right to him."

# CHAPTER FIFTEEN

***FBI Field Office***
***Enterprise St***
***Kapolei, Hawaii***
***October 26th, 2023***
***10:30 A.M.***

BELLA YAWNED AS SHE POURED HERSELF A BLACK COFFEE AND looked toward the conference room. Billy, Keith, and George were diligently reviewing each box. She saw Susan and Rachel in another corner re-checking the files a second time. Bella's own review boxes were scattered over to the left corner where George was picking up the slack while she got a coffee. All the boxes contained every scrap of information they'd rounded up on the Sure-Kill program between the boxes Natalie had produced, Bella's own case files, and the information from the FBI raid in San Diego.

Walking into the conference room, Bella cracked her neck. Then with a tired smile as she sat in her corner, "Good morning, folks."

There were deep yawns followed by stomach grumbles and tired groans. But everyone gave their customary greeting of "Good morning."

It had been four days since Bella and her team put an international manhunt out for Harry Finch. Interpol, NSA, and everyone were on the lookout for the CEO of Yellowrock should his private jet or possibly his private yacht touch down anywhere in the world. The bug they'd placed on Valerie Carrington's phone had been useful in tracking the communications and gathering evidence to rack up dozens of criminal charges, but frustratingly, the mastermind behind the operation was still out there in the wind somewhere.

In the meantime, all the board members and executives of Yellowrock had been served subpoenas, warrants were handed down by FISA to search the stateside warehouses, and all personnel pulled in for questioning by the FBI.

"How's it looking on your side of things, Agent Walker?" Rachel went cross-eyed in the moment as she looked up from her twentieth file.

"I think I hear the Kamikaze Grill calling our names." Bella smirked and did the same cross-eyed gesture. In the same instant Keith and George put their hands out pretending to go blind from all the reading and note-taking. Agent Namara and Agent Makani just shook their heads.

As Bella opened the glass doors to head out to the parking lot with her team, her phone buzzed a text. Bella looked down as she pushed through to go to the parking lot. It was a cryptic text from Aunt Natalie.

*Stay in the building and preferably your office. If you're hungry, order in. The press has swarmed the FBI building like flies.*

Flashes of brilliant camera lighting, camera flashes, and a hundred or more reporters bombarded her instantly. The text had warned too late. Putting her hand up, Bella realized she wasn't the first one hit with questions.

"Is Yellowrock under investigation Agent Roberts?" A pale, paper-thin brown-haired reporter asked.

Natalie herself tried to cover her eyes to answer. "We are involved in an active investigation. We can't say at this time. It could compromise all the hard work my colleagues have done thus far."

A blonde woman with oversized sunglasses and athletic build asked the next question. "Agent Roberts, we have stunning footage of you diving to save a fellow agent who was about to be murdered at a funeral—a funeral coincidentally for Yellowrock investor Alton Lincoln. Was that agent your famous niece Agent Bella Walker?"

At that moment, Bella thought of running back to get out of the camera's view. But she was pinned with her colleagues behind her trying to get back inside as well. As Natalie went to answer, another reporter spotted Bella and the crowd of media journalists ascended on her in a twisting wave forgetting to follow up with Natalie. In the same instant, Natalie took advantage of the moment and bolted back inside the FBI building.

A stocky boulder of a man pushed an ancient microphone into her face before Bella could react and recoil to the sanctuary of the building. "Agent Walker, were you the woman saved by your aunt, Agent Natalie Roberts? How have you fared since your capture of the sadistic Harbinger Serial Killer?"

"I'll answer these two questions, then I have to leave you fine folks and get back to capturing Alton Lincoln and his bride's killer." Bella squinted under the spotlight's glare. She looked at the man's microphone and then out to the growing crowd before answering. "The footage should tell you all you need to know. And to answer the next question, I'm quite well on the peaceful Hawaiian Islands."

Bella heard dozens of more questions being shouted despite her affirmation to only answer two. By this time Keith and a team of agents had pushed through to blockade the reporters. Bella had never been more thankful.

Two questions did irritate her to the point that she turned briefly to answer. They came from a Hawaiian local newsman who had a slight paunch. "Is the FBI going to release a statement on the Alton and Candace Lincoln murders, Agent Walker? What about the international manhunt for Yellowrock CEO Harry Finch?"

Taking a moment to compose her thoughts as she nodded to George and Keith who were keeping the crowd back momentarily. "We will release a statement later this evening. As for Mr. Finch, he's a person of interest in a separate case regarding Yellowrock. At this point he's a person of interest and that's all."

Inside the FBI building, far, far away from the mob of reporters, Charlton Harris was aggravated. "How did the investigation get leaked to the press? The funeral shooting was out on remote Molokai. It takes a year to get groceries on the island, much less any news out of the island. The locals are hush-hush on just about everything."

"In their defense, Director Harris, funeral shootings aren't all that common, sir. Even on the wild west of Molokai." George gave a wide grin and shrugged.

Harris was beyond perturbed. The growing swarm of press and the mounting pressure to close this convoluted case were building. "Are you forever a comic, Agent Dwyer? Because right now I need a tough-as-nails FBI agent and his undaunting team to capture an international killer!"

Bella put a hand on her boss's shoulder to cool his temper. Then she offered a solution. "We'll give a press conference at three o'clock. That should satiate their bloodlust for a little while."

"Both of you will have to give the press conference, Agent Walker." Director Harris looked over to Natalie. "If that's okay by you, FBI legend?"

Natalie gave a mischievous grin. "Now look at who went and tried to be funny. I swear, Agent Dwyer, you are rubbing off on him. We might even get a smile from you again one day, Charlton. Most likely, after the case is closed and you can get back to surfing."

"You know me too well, Agent Roberts."

***FBI Field Office***
***Enterprise St***
***Kapolei, Hawaii***
***October 26th, 2023***
***3:00 P.M.***

Bella groaned just before the press meeting at three o' clock. For starters—to the aggravation of the FBI team—the briefing was delayed by fifteen minutes due to the continued influx of reporters and media still arriving from around the world. Adding to the annoyance was the pushing and shoving of cameramen trying to get in the best position for the best camera angle of the famous duo. Billy and Keith had to pull out handcuffs and remind everyone to act civil.

By three-fifteen, Harris had had enough and nodded to Bella and Natalie to proceed. Before they headed to the podium and cameras, Natalie leaned over and whispered in Bella's ear. "Knock 'em dead, kiddo."

Then she pushed Bella forward into the den of reporters.

It was a surreal moment for Bella. She flashed back to herself as a child with her family. They were watching Aunt Natalie on TV, a tradition in the Walker household. She'd just captured a notorious child predator and been unexpectedly tossed in the spotlight by her boss. Now Bella was being pushed out to speak of their current investigation with Aunt Natalie in the wings to bring additional support to her.

Bella took a breath before walking up to the podium and microphone. She scanned the audience and began. "Thank you for your patience and for coming out today for this debriefing. We are investigating several murders that had appeared at first glance to be performed by a serial killer. But as our investigation proceeded, it has come to our attention that these murders may be part of a highly professional network of assassins that we believe are connected to Yellowrock."

The crowd gasped and whispered, but Bella held both hands up to quell any questions.

"Now, as a separate and concurrent investigation, we have uncovered evidence of illegal experimentation in at least one Yellowrock facility, related to the development of dangerous and unstable biological agents. At this time, we have conducted raids on multiple Yellowrock facilities and taken several executives in custody, who are assisting our investigation. At this time, our top priority is the capture and arrest of Yellowrock's CEO Harry Finch. We ask the local and international communities if you see this man," Bella nodded for the projector screen to display Finch's photo, "to call the FBI hotline immediately." Then Bella, Natalie, and the team began to outline the case briefly and field questions.

Two hours later, and back in the quiet of the conference room, the team were again following up on leads. Sandwiches and coffees had been brought in for the long night ahead reviewing more leads and documents.

"Boy, the more we dig into these, the murkier it gets with Yellowrock." George rubbed his temples then wiped his horn-rimmed glasses clean with a small towelette. "Look at this. Warehouses and weapons depots that link Yellowrock shipments of arms, money, and training personnel to both the Tears of the Dragon and to Arkar Sai's Black Skulls."

Keith tapped a finger over financial records and banking statements. "You can say that again. I have the personal expense accounts from my NSA and IRS contacts. The money they dumped just into Myanmar and that group of Yakuza thugs could have reversed the debt in several struggling nations like, well, Myanmar."

Bella looked at her own box of records, seeing a similar pattern. Putting her hands together, she leaned forward in her chair. "They have been behind much of the recent organized crime activity in Hawaii. Without Yellowrock's money and weapons, the Hawaiian Islands would be far safer."

Billy rushed in with a tray of sandwiches and coffee. He moved with the quickness of a panther, almost spilling the coffee on top of Susan. Exasperated and out of breath he panted, "I just got a tip from one of my confidential informants out on Molokai. Get this, there's a big spender who just landed at the airport in a private chopper. Apparently, he's been trying to pay off the locals for discretion. Anyway, according to what the CI described to me, he fits the description of Yellowrock CEO Harry Finch to a T."

"Where's the suspect now, Agent Makani?" asked Rachel.

Billy pulled a map up on his phone with a pinned direction of the location then linked it to the projector. He then walked up and pointed out the suspect's base and secret compound. "My guy said he and his team took off from the airport heading east on Mauna Loa Highway in three black SUVs. He overheard two of the security personnel talking about the logistical nightmare they were having moving equipment up to their base west of Kalaupapa. But the big tip was when another guy spoke of a compound in the mountains of Kamakou."

Bella looked over to Rachel with a grin as everyone stood to go follow up on Billy's lead. "Another raid in the mountains? We're getting old at these, team. I'm guessing to save time you already booked the flights to Molokai and the hotel?"

Rachel ushered her best friend out the door with the entire assembled team. "Agent Walker, I can see that nothing gets past you."

# CHAPTER SIXTEEN

***Harry Finch Compound***
***Kamakou Mountain***
***Island of Molokai***
***October 29th, 2023***
***06:00A.M.***

RAIN POURED THROUGH THE NIGHT AS BELLA TRIED TO SLEEP. SHE worried if the storms continued that they might have to delay the assault on the possible Finch compound. By three A.M., however, there was a break in the weather. With the assistance of Molokai PD, an additional twenty FBI agents for the mission, and some old friends, the FBI positioned their respective teams for the dangerous assault.

The suspect had been spotted by SWAT surveillance two miles up on the eastern ridge of Kamakou and the location of his hideout had been confirmed over the previous forty-eight hours. All that was left was to bring him in. And luckily for everyone involved, the raid went off without a hitch for once.

It was Rachel and Bravo Team that roared with laughter at the triumphant capture of the suspect. Rachel was winded, but her grin could be heard clear as day through the radio. "All teams, we got him! We have Harry Finch in custody."

"That's great Bravo Team! We need to get him to MPD for a chat. Make sure he stays healthy... and alive." Bella said the words hoping Harry heard them. She wanted to get into his wheelhouse early to get him to squeal. In her experience, the sooner she interviewed him the better before he jammed them up with his team of lawyers.

***Molokai Police Department***
***74-88 Ainoa St***
***Kaunakakai, Hawaii***
***October 29th, 2023***
***11:00 A.M.***

Bella walked into the interview room with two steaming Styrofoam cups in hand. She took a sip of her bitter and burnt coffee and pushed the other over to an athletically built man with raven black, oily hair, and a porcelain white smile. He looked to Bella like he could have come straight out of a movie studio. He kept his finely manicured hands in front of him as he lifted the coffee and winced in distaste to the stuff. Bella said nothing and remained calm and patient waiting for him to speak. Bella wouldn't have to wait long.

Placing the cup down he stayed calm and smoothed out the table with his palms before looking up with his brown eyes. "Thank you for the coffee, Agent—"

"Agent Walker. This is Agent Keith Benton." Bella interrupted Harry, throwing the corrupt executive off guard. And that was the point. She didn't want him to be able to use his charms or rehearsed statements to weasel out of talking. Bella assumed that he had probably memorized a legal speech for just such an occasion to buy time until his lawyers arrived to save the day.

Harry took a deep, controlled breath then turned on the boyish charm. "I'd say it was nice to meet you, but under the circumstances, I'll have to opt out. I think you've arrested the wrong guy. I'm just a paid problem solver out on holiday in these wondrous Hawaiian mountains. I'm not the puppet master here, agents. I'm just another puppet in the machine of Yellowrock."

"Then why not come talk to my boss, SAC Harris, if you had nothing to hide, Mr. Finch?" Keith raised a skeptical brow and adjusted himself in the steel chair. Then he leaned back and crossed his arms waiting on Harry's reply.

Harry slapped his hands together gently. "That's a good question. I'll answer as best I can. You see, the Yellowrock board has protocols—"

Bella was seething at the man's sheer sliminess. "Enough, with the board! We know you deliberately sent assassins out to wipe out your partners and competition," she hissed. "We linked several notable transactions to you through shell companies and offshore accounts in the Philippines, Kathmandu, and Sumatra. We have documents confirming you personally restarted the illegal metagenics program. If that's not enough, we now have several former employees and witnesses that will testify that you ordered several murders across the globe through the Sure-Kill program. Is there anything—anything at all—that you want to say before we throw the book at you, Mr. Finch?"

"How about you get me the best coffee on Molokai?" Finch leaned in, studying their reactions. Bella and Keith didn't give him an inch, but he seemed to take it as good enough. "Then I'll give you every detail, every transaction, and even the real identity of our top killer. But I want assurances that my family will be kept safe, I get full immunity, and that we will all be put into witness protection. Promise me that, and I'll literally give you the keys to the kingdom."

"By the top assassin, you obviously mean Sure-Kill." Keith furrowed his brow and pursed his lips.

Harry frowned and lowered his head for a solemn moment. Bella wasn't buying his charade as he pretended to care. "Yes, the very one. She went rogue and killed our top asset, you know. That's a very lethal lady on the loose."

"She killed English Ivy with her own poison. We know that too, Mr. Finch." Bella raised both her brows and slightly lowered her head.

Finch turned on his devilish charm. "Go ahead and call me Harry. Calling me Mr. Finch makes me feel like you are talking to my father. And… I truly despised my father."

Bella raised a single eyebrow at that. Was the mask slipping? Or was this just another tangled web of lies? For the moment, she decided to play along. "Harry it is. So, here's the deal, Harry. We have you dead to rights on conspiracy to commit murder, illegal genetic research, shipping arms across the globe, and laundering money in at least twenty countries. What could you possibly offer us that we won't eventually figure out on our own?"

Harry's brown eyes seemed to catch fire with a knowledge that chilled Agent Bella Walker and the whole FBI to their very core. When he'd finished speaking, Bella wanted to run out of the room and find a place to hide. "Do you know the number of labs across the world, including the United States, where metagenic delivery systems are being developed"

"What do you mean by that?"

"What I mean is... Yellowrock isn't the only one. Oh, no, far from it. In fact, honestly, the only reason I even started up that lab is because I needed to keep up with the competition."

"Such as?" Bella pressed.

He laughed. "Oh, no. You're not getting it out of me that easily." He tapped a finger on the table. "I want a deal. Now."

"And you can give us all that information, Harry?" Keith was wide-eyed and pale with shock. Bella had never seen the veteran FBI agent so upset.

Harry lifted his brow slightly and gave a mischievous smile. Bella had decided then and there that Harry Finch was indeed the very essence of pure, living evil. And, if there was a God, hopefully she'd find a way to break her deal with this disgusting devil. "Of course I can, Agent Benton. I set up the teams, I ran the day-to-day, I kept the records and logs accurate on everything. I made copies and back-up copies for insurance should a day like today come."

Bella's mouth twitched for a moment as she bit the side of her mouth to keep her composure. What she actually wanted to do was throw this evil man into the darkest cell she could find forever. But what she did instead was play to the arrogant narcissist's ego. "Well, you sound like a man with a wealth of experience and understanding of Yellowrock, Harry. We'd be fools not to give you a deal once your leads pan out. How about a first one on good faith?"

"Sounds great, Agent Walker." He gave a hawkish grin that Bella was certain he'd probably given when he'd ordered Alton Lincoln and Roger Cheney murdered. "Go back to the poisons and follow up with Agent Natalie Roberts... your aunt. There's something she stumbled upon. Something you two might have missed in the way we put the sero-proteins together for the plant adaptogens. Only one company has that particular patent, is all I'll say. Once you find it, crush Yellowrock with it. Start there, and then when you're done, come back. Once that... pans out, I'll take you down another rabbit hole with some pretty interesting tech coming out of Eastern Europe and South Asia."

Bella pushed back from her chair, unsteady at what Harry had just revealed. Not only was their case evolving in its understanding of the techniques Yellowrock had implemented over several decades of assassinations, but Finch was also telling them of future dangerous biological weapons that could come from anywhere across the globe.

As Bella and Keith walked into the next room shaking their bewildered heads, they glanced toward a stunned and nervous FBI team.

*Harry Finch is smiling and telling me all the answers. But I know he's a liar, a master manipulator, and more than likely a sadistic man who gets off on driving fear and pain into others. And that from just a few hours of our interview.*

*Let's hope he's all fluff and just taking the FBI for a ride. But I can't help but feel Harry Finch was just showing off how truly evil he really is.*

***Hotel Molokai***
***1300 Kamehameha V Highway***
***Kaunakakai, Hawaii***
***October 29th, 2023***
***17:00 P.M.***

It had been a long, exhausting day as Bella made her way through the lobby of her hotel. She'd long sent the rest of the team back for needed showers and rest after the assault and subsequent interrogation of Harry Finch. Moving with an all-around muscle stiffness that only a steaming hot shower could fix, Bella lumbered out to her room.

But Harry Finch's words about the key to toppling Yellowrock were stuck in her head.

*Go back to the poisons and follow up with Agent Natalie Roberts… your aunt. There's something she stumbled upon.*

Bella took a deep, haggard breath and detoured to Natalie's room. She knocks gently hoping that her aunt was still wide awake. She wasn't too surprised after her third and fourth series of knocks that her aging aunt wasn't responding.

*Aunt Natalie must be out like a light. I'm about to be, too.*

Bella turned and stepped away without making any more noise. A sound made her pause. She waited to hear it again, then shrugged and was about to walk off when the sound came fainter.

It was gasping on the other side of Natalie's door!

"Aunt Natalie!"

Bella threw her body into Natalie's door, but it wouldn't budge. She launched two kicks, splintering the molding and breaking the door's lock. Moving with the fury of a hurricane, Bella felt her heart stop as she froze in her tracks for just an instant to witness a terrifying sight.

There, foaming at the mouth on the floor, was the writhing and twisting form of Aunt Natalie. With her eyes rolled back, sheets of sweat falling from her face, and the woman's bowels voided, Bella recognized her beloved aunt was in the deadly throes of a seizure.

# CHAPTER SEVENTEEN

Aunt Natalie was seizing! She had no history of epilepsy or any malady. It could only be one thing—poison.

Bella rushed to the floor and pulled her aunt's head up from the floor before she hurt herself, quickly whipping her head left and right in search of a first aid kit. Then she saw it: Natalie's open bag on the floor, which contained the yellow epinephrine pen handed out to the FBI team by Dr. Wecht. Bella scrambled over to grab it, quickly popped the safety cap, and slammed the autoinjector into Natalie's left upper thigh.

In seconds the seizure stopped. Watching her aunt carefully, Bella waited to see if the dose of the epi had been enough. The time ticked like hours as Bella called for emergency services and watched her aunt. She prayed as she hugged Aunt Natalie, that she wouldn't need to deliver a second dose.

Barely a few minutes later, as the ambulance arrived, Bella was thankful that only one had been enough to save her aunt. She had come to a little but was still weak and groggy.

With her voice a frail, tired whisper, Aunt Natalie reached for a crying Bella's hand. "That... was close, Bella. Thank you."

"It's what we do, you know," Bella managed through tears, echoing what Natalie had said to her not too long ago. Bella hugged her aunt with a sob as EMS loaded her into the unit.

The paramedic nodded to Bella as he climbed in the back with Aunt Natalie. "We'll get her over to the E.R. right away. You saved her life, you know."

Bella nodded numbly then climbed in with her aunt and the medic. She hugged her Aunt Natalie again for the trip as he checked her vitals, adjusted Aunt Natalie's IV, and checked the EKG monitor.

***Molokai General Hospital***
***Emergency Room***
***280 Home Olu Place***
***Kaunakakai, Hawaii***
***October 30th, 2023***
***01:00 A.M.***

Bella hadn't left Aunt Natalie's side for one moment throughout the examination and follow-up histories with the E.R. physician Dr. Cameron Lowery.

The gangly, balding doctor with worn blue eyes listened intently to Bella's recollections of what had happened and her use of epinephrine to counteract the poison cocktail. As Bella finished her explanation in between the lab, x-ray, and other technicians arriving to get samples from her aunt, Dr. Lowery acknowledged, "It goes without saying, you saved her life. We'll keep her overnight for observation, but all the reports say she's fit as a fiddle."

"Dr. Lowery, I prefer to be called fit as a violin." Aunt Natalie rolled her eyes as Dr. Lowery shrugged with a sheepish smile and wandered off.

"Are you, okay Bella?" Rachel had arrived with the entire FBI team. She went up and hugged Bella as did the whole team in a group hug.

"I'm—" Bella tried to steel her nerves and not cry. She failed on all accounts and teared up for just a moment. Then she composed herself. "I'm fine now. I wasn't so good when she was seizing. Dr. Wecht's pen saved her life."

"No, dear. You using Dr. Wecht's pen saved Natalie's life. Own it, Agent Walker. You thought quickly and saved her life." Keith was stern as the whole team continued to group hug their lead investigator.

"Alright, back to work, you knuckleheads. Besides you guys are suffocating me with all this corniness." Bella wiped her tears and glanced as Aunt Natalie blew her a kiss on her way to the room. Bella ushered them over to the waiting room as the hospital floor team transported Aunt Natalie to her observation room.

George asked the obvious next question as the team huddled in chairs next to a dirty window. "Do you think it was Sure-Kill?"

Bella looked forward a moment then shrugged. "The probability is high that she was. But with an outfit as evil as Yellowrock with a bullpen of killers, we need to know with certainty."

Keith rubbed his chin as he looked over to Bella with stern eyes. "It's Occam's Razor here, I think. Don't overthink it. The most likely killer—who has history with your aunt—is probably the killer."

Susan walked up and hugged Bella in the waiting room. With tears flowing from her eyes, she added, "I'm so sorry for what happened to your aunt, Agent Walker."

"Thank you, Susan." Bella caught something in the young blonde's lithe, porcelain hand and pointed to it, puzzled. "What's that?"

Susan pushed the object to Bella and excitedly stammered. "I found this behind the desk in the room. She must have tossed it when she seized."

In her hand was a map.

# CHAPTER EIGHTEEN

***Hotel Molokai***
***1300 Kamehameha V Highway***
***Kaunakakai, Hawaii***
***October 31st, 2023***
***08:00 A.M.***

A warm breeze gusted from the sea and up toward Bella as she sat looking at a fog-filled early morning. She and her team sat at an outside table overlooking the Molokai coastline. Natalie, feeling one hundred percent better though a little shaky at times, was at the head of the table. Everyone had gathered early to review every step and detail prior to her poisoning.

Keith sat nearest to Natalie. Everyone was still shaken up by the attack on one of their own. Everyone shared the same concern for self-preservation with the thinking that if Sure-Kill could get the drop on Natalie Roberts… then anyone was fair game. "So, from what you are telling me, you didn't run or bump into anybody, Agent Roberts? You didn't notice any type of bee sting or dart?"

"Well, now that you mention it, Agent Benton, there was something." Aunt Natalie pushed back a curl of her graying hair. "I felt a sting, like a minor mosquito bite. But it was after I was in my room, which is quite troubling. I'm usually meticulous about my room and even have fail safes in play to warn me if someone has entered it while I was out. How they got past those bothers me intensely. As I'm sure all of you are concerned for your own safety."

"How do we safeguard against a poisoner who got past you, Agent Roberts? I mean you are always so intense on details like someone else we know at the table." Susan nodded over to Bella as the team chuckled. Then Susan put her elbows on the table and her head in her hands with a groan. She seemed more than troubled by the possibility of being poisoned.

Natalie smiled slightly and gave Bella a proud look. "As an FBI agent, always be on guard, is all I can say." Aunt Natalie sighed and looked toward the Hotel Molokai with a furrowed brow and a narrowed stare. "As for now, and here on until we catch Sure-Kill, watch your back, be vigilant, and wash everything—hands, feet, and the like, frequently. I don't have a doubt in my mind that she was the one responsible for this."

George took a sip of a steaming cup of tea then asked, "From the sound of things, Agent Roberts, it sounds like you might have caught Sure-Kill in your room and startled her. It's probably one of the reasons you're still with us. The other, of course, is Bella showed up when she did."

"He's got a point," Bella said. "She's not called Sure-Kill for nothing. She must have got thrown out of her routine to finish off her target—you. Either you startled her while she was looking for something, or I ran her off when I just happened to show up. Either prospect is chilling to think about, though."

"That seems quite plausible." Aunt Natalie placed her hands on the table and interlocked them before continuing. "And, I have to agree, Bella, quite terrifying to know that she was seconds from wrapping up my career permanently."

"I have to ask, Nat. What's the deal with the Molokai map Agent Namara found?" Keith pointed to the map on the table in front of them.

"I was perusing over it. This was in Alton Lincoln's suitcase for some reason." Bella furrowed her brow, wondering how Aunt Natalie had made time to search through the dead man's things. "I can see by the puzzlement of everyone, you want to know why."

Bella narrowed her eyes and spoke sternly. "You didn't share that you had found this with anyone, Aunt Natalie. That's not how a team usually does things."

"My apologies, everyone, for not telling you sooner. I stumbled on it when we were double checking all the items. The guy had sewn it in the suitcase lining. It was not a very good sewing job if you don't mind me saying, as I saw a piece of the map reflecting between the threads." Aunt Natalie sighed as she looked down on the color-coded map. "I must have dropped it behind the desk when Sure-Kill struck."

Bella leaned in next to Aunt Natalie and put her chin on her hand. The map was an oddity for the FBI sleuth. Its dimensions were a discreet thirty inches wide and ten inches in height with folds that could render the map six inches wide with the worn creases. The image on the map was of the island of Molokai with specific island markers used as reference. But the peculiar thing that stood out to all was the map's legend. Astrological markings and colored locations meant something to the user of the map.

Scratching his head and looking out to the Molokai mountain range and then back to the map, Billy asked, "If I'm seeing these right, Agent Roberts, those astrological signs in the legend correspond to the color schematic in some way across various points of the island. What do they mean?"

Aunt Natalie rubbed her temples then her eyes trying to focus on the map. "That's where I was at with this wacky thing when I got dosed by Sure-Kill. Near-death got in the way of me deciphering this thing."

Bella leaned back and crossed her arms. Lowering her head and grimacing, "The astrological symbols are obvious Zodiac references." Bella leaned back in and pointed as the team followed her lead. "That part is easy enough. The color codes must be specific locations that meant something to do with his defense meetings or specific projects. Maybe particular business deals—he was effectively a salesman, after all. But why the code? Why the secrecy?"

The manager of the Hotel Molokai—a tall, thin Hawaiian man named Tommy Hai—walked up timidly deciding whether to interrupt the FBI team. Bella could see the man was indecisive and ushered him over. "My apologies for interrupting, agents. We have the surveillance recording ready for you."

"Thank you, Tommy. Let's go have a look." Bella ushered everyone toward the manager's office.

Initially the grain on the security display was a little dark. Tommy adjusted the color and increased the contrast. The figure of a housekeeper, who hardly looked like any of Tommy's staff with her height and athletic build, seemed to move like a panther into Natalie's room without her cart. The housekeeper seemed to shuffle about Natalie's room looking for something. She rummaged through her aunt's suitcase and under her pillows before stomping her foot in a rage. Then the intruding woman seemed to spy something on the desk by the window. The housekeeper was leaping to grab the color-coded map when Natalie unlocked the door. With a sudden turn of the head, the woman slinked back into the shadows as Natalie entered the room and headed straight for the desk, to grab the map herself.

The next scene was too difficult for Natalie to continue to watch. Bella put an arm around her as she winced watching Sure-Kill slinking in to poison her. Luckily or not, in the heat of the moment, Natalie had rocked back seizing. The seizure motion had a twofold effect. First, it caused Natalie to careen backward into Sure-Kill before she could inject the full dose. With the killer blinded by her own blood and her head stunned by the blow, Sure-Kill didn't see in the same instant that Natalie's seizure and falling back caused the map to fall behind the desk.

In the next frames of the video, Bella was seen knocking several times on Aunt Natalie's door. This further disrupted Sure-Kill's opportunity to finish off Aunt Natalie and find the map. The next frame showed the moment Bella crashed through the door, while Sure-Kill jumped out the hotel window to flee.

"I don't know about the rest of you, but I got chills watching that." Rachel shook herself and crossed both her arms trying to warm up.

"You can say that again," Natalie murmured.

# CHAPTER NINETEEN

***Molokai Police Department***
***74-88 Ainoa St***
***Kaunakakai, Hawaii***
***October 31st, 2023***
***10:00 A.M.***

"THE SHEER HUBRIS OF THAT CORRUPT GROUP, TO DISREGARD the rule of law, is disgusting!" Aunt Natalie roared as they drove to the MPD. She seemed to clinch her hands tightly as she seethed in a rage. "These people always think they are above the law."

As MPD Officer Maena made a bouncing turn on the outskirts of town, Bella added, "I'm just as outraged, Aunt Natalie. I feel so utterly helpless and useless right now knowing that Sure-Kill is still out in the jungle after she almost killed you. Then these other horrific thoughts—"

Aunt Natalie narrowed her green eyes. "What thoughts, Bella Walker?"

Bella looked up, pausing before she continued. She shook her head then confessed. "I had some hang-ups right after the video of you almost being killed. It triggered a recollection from Agent Shelley's machine. A Candace Kincaid or Alton Lincoln memory from that crackpot's brain scrambler. It was brief and has passed."

Wide-eyed in disbelief, Aunt Natalie scolded her reckless niece again for ever having volunteered to be Victor Shelley's guinea pig. "You see why you should never volunteer, miss! I warned you—"

"Never again, I swear." Bella interrupted and put her hand up. She made a playful, solemn face and a Girl Scout promise sign with her hand. Aunt Natalie scowled and shook her head. "We need to get down to solving this map. I hate to tell you this Aunt Natalie, knowing how fond you are of that mad scientist's invention. But I think one of those memories may help us crack the map."

"Never again, Bella!" she repeated. "And if this dead victim's memory does help us on the case, you will never tell anyone that the Ghost-in-the-Machine was why."

Bella nodded in agreement.

Walking up with the rest of the team, Bella nodded over to Rachel and Keith before walking inside the department. "Once we figure this map out, I think we need another round with Harry Finch."

The door opened and a tall, tanned man with eyes the color of a roaring wave opened the door for his agents. "Ladies and gentlemen, it's damn glad to see all of you this fine Molokai morning. I figured I'd fly out in person to check up on all of you."

"That's so kind SAC Harris. But what's the real reason, sir?" Keith gave his boss a knowing grin. Then pointed to the North Shore of Molokai.

"Guilty as charged, Agent Benton. Let's wrap this one up today, shall we?" Director ushered everyone in and added, "Agent Roberts, I was going to ask Agent Walker this question after her round with the Ghost-in-the-Machine. But since you one-upped her, how was it coming back from the dead?"

"Not funny, Charlton. Not funny one bit." But Natalie laughed despite herself.

Harris put his hands up defensively. "Someone trying to kill you is never funny. I jumped right on the jet when I heard. I'm glad you are okay, Natalie."

Bella realized something profound in her boss's flushed face.

*He dropped everything to fly to Molokai because Aunt Natalie was almost killed. It wasn't to surf Molokai. He had plenty of surf spots on Oahu and Kauai for that.*

"You really do care, SAC Harris," she teased.

The man broke into a grin. "Guilty as charged."

"Come on back. We've got a big briefing this morning."

With everyone seated, Bella began. She passed out photocopies of the map and began detailing the various color schemes of each island location and referencing the astrological charts and constellations. She pointed to each mountain or coastal spot highlighted and explained the connection to the legend and each symbol. Then she recalled Alton's grinning memory showing Candace what he'd created so she could find him whenever she needed him."

"Alton Lincoln made this map for Candace to locate him anytime on the job. He was concerned that something might happen to him, so he left it for the love of his life." Bella lowered her head, trying to push the smiling man, with the mischievous boyish grin, out of her head. "You see, his friend, fellow Yellowrock associate Roger Cheney, had reached out to him. We don't know why Cheney suddenly developed a conscience. But before Sure-Kill got to him, he passed along the information he'd uncovered to Alton. We all know it now—the metagenic research, the secret facilities, all that stuff we're already wrapping up Yellowrock with. Shortly after passing along that information to Alton, Roger disappeared. Alton was afraid he'd be next, that something might happen, so he made this map for Candace."

"There's irony for you, Agent Walker. He did it for Candace so she wouldn't worry about him. And the minute he did this map, Yellowrock sanctioned her to kill him. Maybe if she doesn't report Alton's massive screw-up, they both sail off into the sunset." George leaned forward shaking his head.

Keith added as he sat back in his chair. "Or Sure-Kill eliminates them both anyway. Seems anyone working in the upper management for Yellowrock sooner or later ends up on a cold morgue slab." Keith ran his fingers through his graying hair.

SAC Harris walked up and looked over the original map carefully. Then pointed. "So, the constellations align with the months that each warehouse or compound is active. The astrological signs tell you which compound house guns, projects, and personnel. Both have to align here for the color-coding to match." Crossing his arms and rubbing his chin with his right hand. "This is great work team. I've never seen such insight into a victim's psyche, Agent Walker. What did you tap into to solve this map?"

Natalie rolled her eyes at her niece, giving her a warning glare. With Charlton's back turned, she mouthed, "Not a word about the toy."

Bella took a deep breath and shrugged. "I was able to put it together based on some of the information we received from the FBI raids over on the mainland." It wasn't a complete lie, after all.

"So, what's our next move here?" Harris asked.

"With the subpoenas and cases racking up back on the mainland, you can bet Yellowrock's illegal operations will ramp up on Molokai. They'll be shifting personnel, weapons, and everything out of the main headquarters and moving it here and here." Bella pointed to the mountainous areas on the map. "I'm guessing this is the temporary hub for their operations until they get set up on their own island somewhere in the Pacific."

Rachel stood and studied the assault locations before turning to face the team. "Looks like we'll be proceeding with the assault in the next six hours. Time to round up the gang."

Harris gave a broad grin sitting forward in his chair. He studied everyone carefully before saying off-cuff, "Well, we have a few hours to kill. I'd sure like to finally meet Yellowrock CEO Harry Finch. Maybe we get him to sing again. Agent Gentry, you accompany me in the briefing while Agent Walker makes her observation." He looked over to Bella. "See if you can pinpoint each of his lies if you can, Agent Walker. Most of what he'll say will be what we want to hear. Like a used car salesman trying to sell a clunker. But we just might catch a break and there may be some truth in his twisted tales."

Raising her left brow skeptically, Bella took a long sigh. "Let's hope so, sir. But he's one of the best liars and manipulators that I've seen in a long time."

Bella walked with Rachel and Harris to MPD's briefing area. Waiting in the observation room studying Harry Finch behind a mirrored glass, she nodded over to Chief Tagomori who also was in attendance.

"Special Agent in Charge Harris! It's so good to finally meet you." Harry Finch gave a jovial smile as he sat at an interview table with his hands cuffed in front and to chains attached to the steel table. He stuck out both his cuffed hands to shake.

Unpersuaded and undaunted by Harry's smile and demeanor, Bella got to see the wizened FBI agent at his sleuth best. It was no wonder he'd risen up the ranks at such a historically young age. "Your gang almost killed some of the FBI's best agents. And more importantly to your longevity—you tried killing one of my best friends. So, either your orders got botched or you didn't know Sure-Kill would risk more Yellowrock exposure in an already pressure cooker of a situation for the company. Which exactly is it, Mr. Finch?"

Harry lowered his head and grimaced in disgust. He slammed his right hand down on the MPD metal table before him angrily. Then he looked up slightly and met eyes with SAC Harris. "Tatiana Morozova."

Rachel widened her brown eyes slightly asking, "Who's Tatiana Morozova?"

Harry Finch rubbed his forehead with his left hand as best he could. Then he advised the team to everyone's surprise. "Sure-Kill's real name. I never tolerate insubordination. Her orders were clear to stay low, and she disobeyed my specific instructions to not kill any more agents on my watch."

"Thanks for assisting the FBI, Mr. Finch. It'll go a long way to us helping you with your plea-bargaining deal." Harris nodded to Rachel, who looked surprised that he was cutting the interview short.

Once they were back out of the room, Rachel had to ask. "Sir, that had to be one of the shortest interviews in history. He was just getting ready to spill the beans on the whole operation. What gives?"

"He gave me what I needed to know. We have to leave this guy guessing and off-balance to crack him." Charlton sighed as he recalled something before he continued. "He was too quick to give up Sure-Kill's real name. Which tells me there's a plan in play that we aren't seeing. Maybe it's DoJ or DoD favoring him to get himself immunity. But unfortunately for him, now I know for certain he orchestrated the attempted murder on Agent Roberts, and he more or less openly admitted to ordering the hits on all of Sure-Kill's targets. Rest assured, there is absolutely zero way he gets out of this one."

"Famous last words, Harris," replied Bella. She understood what her boss was getting at, but that didn't mean she had to like it.

***Molokai Airport***
***Hoolehua, Hawaii***
***October 31st, 2023***
***18:35 P.M.***

In an office building adjacent to the airport, Bella, George, and Rachel began setting up desks, moving tables, and putting out pictures and documents for the incoming three hundred personnel that comprised the FBI's assault on the Yellowrock compounds. After setting up the last chair and last picture, Bella looked up to see SAC Harris decked out in full black military BDUs. He had driven out with Chief Tagomori to shuffling and meeting with the first of the military assault and SWAT teams coming from Oahu.

Walking up to the rest of his core FBI group, Harris looked over to Bella and nodded. "Everyone will be here in the next hour. Make sure they know how lethal Sure-Kill is with her poisons. We definitely don't want a repeat poisoning."

"No, we definitely do not, sir." Bella nodded as she, Natalie, and Rachel set up the projector and checked the lighting and presentation images on the screen.

By seven o'clock, all three hundred personnel for the Yellowrock assault had arrived. Bella began her meeting walking up to a makeshift podium next to the projection screen. She carefully canvassed the room looking at the intense and focused eyes of the team personnel, smiling briefly at the familiar faces in the crowd.

"Good evening, folks. I want to start by thanking you for your committed dedication in capturing criminals across the Hawaiian Islands. Many of the faces in this audience are quite familiar to me from the Jade Princess and War Gods cases. For the new personnel, I'm Agent Bella Walker, lead agent for our latest target." Bella nodded as Rachel put up the picture of Sure-Kill. "This is Sure-Kill, possibly named Tatiana Morozova. She's the top assassin for the defense contractor Yellowrock. Consider her extremely dangerous, the most dangerous target we've faced yet."

After fifteen minutes of debriefing the team on Yellowrock and Sure-Kill, Bella took the names given her by the leaders of each of the assault divisions. While the personnel waited patiently, Bella, Rachel, and Harris went through the process of setting up the assault teams and their leadership.

As was always her pre-assault routine, Bella performed her usual checks before the big field meeting at the base camp north of Kalaupapa. She adjusted the straps on her bulletproof vest as she moved with her colleagues to assault transport helicopters. From the base camp, the team would move to surround the compound on the Kalaupapa Peninsula using SEAL fast attack boats pushing from the sea to blockade any boats attempting to leave. Helicopters and airport lockdowns would prevent any trying to escape by plane. It would hopefully be a strategic sweep west, east, north, and south of the peninsula from six locations to close any gaps that might allow Sure-Kill and the Yellowrock rogues from escaping.

Alpha Team was led by none other than Lieutenant Chuck Child. The golden haired, towering titan had worked with Bella on several assault assignments. Today's mission would have Alpha Team in a Vector attack helicopter moving from the western side of Kalaupapa Peninsula.

Bravo Team, assigned to Rachel and Captain Clancy Straub, would approach in helicopters from the eastern side of Kalaupapa Peninsula trying to stop Yellowrock's mercenaries from an airport or jungle escape. Their mission would be to blockade any naval escapes and to surround Kalaupapa by attack craft. Once the blockade was in place, Rachel's team would come ashore and surround from the north.

Agent George Dwyer and Sergeant Owen Ashton headed up Charlie Team with two platoons from Marine Reconnaissance. Charlie Team's mission would push northeast from the sea via combat craft assault vehicles. The boats would provide a cover and blockade as they approached to drop off George and Charlie Team for the beach assault.

Agents Billy Makani and Keith Benton were assigned to Delta Team with Rear Admiral Drew Reynolds from the US Coast Guard, where they would approach from the western seaside of Kalaupapa Peninsula trying to stop Yellowrock's mercenaries from a naval escape, working in conjunction with Charlie Team.

Finally, Natalie Roberts and Susan Namara were assigned to Echo Team, with assistance from a newcomer: Master Chief Petty Officer Kristin Sullivan from the Navy. She was a hardcore, no-nonsense woman, and Bella warmed to her immediately as she introduced herself. This team would sweep behind Alpha and Bravo teams making sure no Yellowrock mercenaries and personnel got past the teams and into the caves and lava tube systems. No one wanted a repeat manhunt of trekking through those, especially Bella after her last—near fatal—misadventure in them.

There was one FBI team member who was on the fence about joining the assault out in the field. Mostly because he still carried the lead from their last mission in Kauai. In the end, SAC Harris roared at the basecamp tent in Kalaupapa, "Alright, team, gather up. Let's run through the missions of each team one more time!"

# CHAPTER TWENTY

***FBI Yellowrock Assault Basecamp***
***Kalaupapa, Hawaii***
***October 31st, 2023***
***22:00 P.M.***

Cool winds seemed to blast the base camp as Bella ran through her second assault presentation. "Her name is Tatiana Morozova. She was born in a small town in the Carpathian Mountains."

Captain Clancy Straub interrupted to bring a little levity to the tense group. "Agent Walker, don't tell us we're chasing a vampire on Halloween Night!" The members of the assault team bellowed with laughter while grabbing their necks jokingly.

"I knew one of you would catch the reference to the Carpathians and go full Dracula on me." Bella rolled her eyes and snickered… a little. "No, she's far worse than a bloodsucker, Captain. She's one of the deadliest assassins in the world. Her preferred method of killing is a new state-of-the-art poisoning system using metagenic technology. Please be extremely cautious if you spot her. I won't say shoot to kill. But in her case…" Bella shrugged with a stern stare. "Anyway, her codename is Sure-Kill for a reason. Two hundred suspected eliminated targets, including her former protégé and recent rival, English Ivy."

Bella nodded as Billy ran the next set of images on the projector. "Our investigation has confirmed that Sure-Kill was essentially the leader of the entire network of assassins employed by Yellowrock and doing freelance work on the side. We still have a lot to uncover, but we have no idea of the forces and methods she has at her disposal. And that's before we even get to the other Yellowrock agents."

Bella talked briefly of the targets and the methods they were found murdered by Sure-Kill. There wasn't any more laughing or frivolity after her presentation. And that had been the point of waiting until they reached base camp. SAC Harris had made it clear to Bella to scare the hell out of the personnel, so no one let their guard down out in the field. "Are there any questions before we move to compound breach—"

Four black-tinted windowed hummers pulled up, moving fast. The teams reacted with everyone turning on a dime and raising their firearms. Bella herself had dropped to one knee with her pistol drawn. Two groups of militant-looking men armed with military-issue AR-15s exited the vehicle aligned in two tight columns. They wore black fatigues that held a yellow, sun-like crest on their right arms—the logo of Yellowrock's mercenary division. All the men's uniforms were sharply pressed and creased. Combat boots, brass rank insignia, and military bearing highly polished and precise, they stared down the team.

The apparent leader barked out for his men to branch into two aligned formations and drop to a knee with their rifles raised to fire. Then the commander—Commander Swanson, according to his sewn name tag—and his second in command, Sergeant Howard, approached the tent just as lightning flashed and a pitter of rain began to fall. Bella, unimpressed and unmoved, kept her pistol on both.

"FBI agents and assault teams, stand down!" Commander Swanson ordered with a menacing command. "I don't know what got in your minds to arrest us, but it won't go as planned. We are a defense company that works directly with your intelligence community."

"Seems to me like you're criminals at best and committing treason at worst," fired back SAC Harris. "What is the meaning of this?"

Sergeant Howard cast his hazel eyes carefully around the group of armed police, military, and SWAT teams. He seemed to take a cooler approach than his commander. "Look, we are just like you. We follow our orders, pay our taxes, and work with your departments to keep America safe from foreign and domestic enemies at all costs."

"Then why kill your own?" Harris stood, but whispered to Rachel, "If he shoots me, kill all of them. I don't plan on getting shot, but my luck lately hasn't been that good." She and Bella both furrowed their brows in a warning not to go forward. "I'm Special Agent in Charge Harris of the Hawaii FBI. I'm the lead commander of this mission. I am standing to discuss your surrender. Anyone shoots me, these kind folks behind me will light you up like the fourth of July. Are we clear, Commander Swanson and Sergeant Howard?"

"Crystal clear, sir." Commander Swanson answered back then pointed to his men. "But we won't be surrendering to –"

A powerful hand—a hand that could have belonged to the giant Goliath himself—grabbed Commander Swanson by his neck in the darkness, lifting him off his feet. A second set of aged, leathered hands—like those of a pirate—had moved a blade to the throat of Sergeant Howard and ripped his gun from him. Both men were displayed to their terrified men.

Bella smiled radiantly as the hulking man growled a warning to the Yellowrock mercenaries. "You are surrounded right now by an entire platoon of special warfare members eager to open fire. I can crack your commander's neck right now. Or you can drop your weapons and lay flat on the ground, face down with your arms out. Are we clear?"

There was a tense moment—a minute at best—where Bella thought there might be a gun battle. Then one by one the Yellowrock mercenaries dropped their weapons and surrendered. Chief Justin Trestle threw the leader to the ground with a thud. Rachel immediately directed the team to move forward and begin the arrests.

Bella ran up and gave her fiancée a well-deserved hug and kiss. Aunt Natalie moved up wide-eyed as well to thank him and huff scoldingly at… Algernon Magnum.

"What took you so long?" Aunt Natalie fussed Algernon as he shoved Sergeant Howard over to Keith who cuffed the mercenary leader.

"What took so long? I had to wake my first mate Rusty out of a drunken coma. When that didn't work, I was left training this big lug in a literal fly-by-night to get here. And don't get me started on the landing." Algernon shrugged as Aunt Natalie almost heaved in happiness as she embraced the old sailor. With a tear in his eye that he wiped before Aunt Natalie saw, "I got word the day after you got out of the hospital. Are… are… you—"

"I'm fine, Algae." Aunt Natalie gave her own hug and kiss to the other man who saved their lives.

"See, I told you, you couldn't kill bad grass, Chief Trestle," he squawked.

Bella and both men laughed as Aunt Natalie scolded Algernon playfully then swatted him.

"Did you really have a team surrounding them?" Bella whispered.

Justin grinned and held out his hands wide. "Well. We may have exaggerated a little. But ain't that the pirate life?"

Bella groaned. "Leave it to the two of you to cook up some crazy scheme. But don't you ever pull a stunt like that again, you hear me?"

"Aye..." Justin said cheekily. He produced an eyepatch and pirate hat out of nowhere and quickly slipped them on. "But no promises," he added in a pirate voice, making Bella crack up.

"Alright you two. Thanks for the last-minute save. Now, Aunt Natalie and I have a villain to catch." Bella released Justin and headed to the teams who had finished the last of the round-ups of the Yellowrock mercenaries. She turned with the biggest of grins. "Justin, go home and take care of my dog!"

Algernon hollered to both ladies as he ushered Justin back home. "That's gratitude for you, Chief Trestle. The things I swear you do out of love. Have a safe FBI assault, agents. And Happy Halloween!"

Aunt Natalie froze in her tracks and turned abruptly wide-eyed and wide mouthed to Algernon. "Algernon Magnum, did you finally get the courage to say what I think you said after twenty damn years?"

# CHAPTER TWENTY-ONE

***Kalaupapa Peninsula***
***Kalaupapa, Hawaii***
***November 1st, 2023***
***01:00 A.M.***

WITH THE TEAMS MOBILIZING ON THE HELICOPTERS AND FAST attack boats, SAC Harris made an ominous statement about a lurid possibility, "If their own mercenaries got tipped off we were coming, what's to say the remnants of Yellowrock and Sure-Kill haven't flown the coop?"

"That may be a possibility." Rachel winced as she admitted it. "Sure-Kill might have escaped already by private jet or yacht, and we'd be none the wiser."

"George, Billy, what do you think? Is it possible this is an exercise in futility?" Bella pointed out to the mustering teams headed to their respective locations to begin the assault. She was getting ready to head out when she, too, asked.

George crossed his arms and looked out toward the coastline then surveyed the jungle canopy of Kalaupapa. "The airports and docks have been under twenty-four-hour surveillance by manned personnel, security cameras, and even drones. I'm not going to one hundred percent rule out Sure-Kill or her cronies couldn't have escaped, especially if they had some type of high-tech submarine, but I don't see it being likely."

Billy looked toward everyone with a raised right brow as he scratched his chin. "I followed up on the submarines as well with Chief Sullivan and Lieutenant Child. Based on their Navy intel, no submarines, or manned ROVs have been spotted by sonar or any of their current surveillance techniques. I also checked any possible fast attack craft or hover ships. Yes, hovercraft are a new means of escape—who knew?"

Bella groaned at the other possible craft and weaponry. "I checked their books and invoices, Agent Makani. They have hovers and UAPs at one of their locations. Let's hope it isn't this one." She shrugged, "But you're correct, gentlemen. There's been no sign of them leaving or bringing on extra troops since we shut down their travel."

"Well, it's settled then, we head out." Harris walked with George to catch a ride with Charlie Team. Bella sent a quick prayer for her boss that he wouldn't get shot this time around.

*Director Harris is a great boss. But he takes too many risks sometimes with his life. Like someone else I know.*

Another familiar face hiked up to Bella carrying a drone console. He was a stocky man with graying brown hair and blue eyes set behind fogged glasses. With a tight grin, he adjusted his HPD Drone Team short-sleeved shirt as he spoke. "Agent Walker, we meet again in such lovely splendor."

"Sergeant Garret Patrick, our last outing was way too short." Bella spoke sarcastically with a wry grin. The leader of the HPD drone division shook back as well. As always, Bella had specifically requested Sergeant Patrick's expertise for this assignment. "These are the latest and greatest toys for the operation."

"Agent Walker, can I speak with you?" A shouting Chief Tagomori of MPD cut in. He hurriedly ran to Bella as she and Sergeant Patrick were making strides toward her team's helicopter.

Bella shouted back with an annoyed glance. "If you hurry, Chief Tagomori. I have a helicopter to catch."

"The winds are moving too fast from the northwest to bring the drones in. Might I suggest your drone guy launch them from the northeast and use the gusts of Kamakou Volcano to push the drones in a more controlled and faster surveillance to the compound. It'll save time for the helicopter transports as well, I might add."

Exasperated, Bella exclaimed as Chief Tagomori red-faced shrugged his apology. "And now you tell me, Chief!"

***Kalaupapa Peninsula***
***Kalaupapa, Hawaii***
***November 1st, 2023***
***02:00 A.M.***

One hour after Chief Tagomori gave the time saving information for Bella and the FBI assault teams, Bella's chopper was on the perimeter of the Yellowrock compound. She crackled her radio. "Drone Team, what's the status of the compound?"

"Drones canvassing the perimeter are now moving in," replied Sergeant Patrick. There was a pause while the teams all waited at each of their locations to advance. "All teams, Yellowrock targets spotted west of the compound gates. There appears to be at least thirty personnel led by what looks like the woman Sure-Kill. She's in battle fatigues leading the group. Repeat, Yellowrock targets spotted west of the compound gates."

Bella excitedly went to order the final push to capture Sure-Kill and her Yellowrock thugs. "You heard—"

Sergeant Patrick screamed in a panic interrupting Bella's order. "Drone under attack by… something! It… it looks like a UAP, UFO, or hell, I don't know what this thing is!"

SAC Harris came over the radio trying to calm the edgy drone operator. "Take a breath, Sergeant. For starters get the drones out of there. Then say again what you just saw."

"It's some kind of massively fast, silver cylinder. It's the size of a police drone but I've never seen anything move like that. It just flew up from the compound warehouse, sir. Wait, the woman Sure-Kill is directing it for another attack on the drones." Sergeant Patrick seemed out of breath as he yelled in a panic. "It's circling to strike the drones!"

Bella and the team watched stunned at the advanced unidentified aerial phenomenon, and the speed it was coursing to obviously destroy the drones. Helpless, she watched as the silver sphere was seconds from wiping out the assault team's valued eyes in the sky.

*It has to be some type of zero energy propulsion to move and turn that quickly. We'll be going into this assault virtually blind if that thing crashes our drones.*

Suddenly—whether by providence or just dumb luck—Bella watched the UAP twist and head downward. Instantly it crashed with a blinding explosion into the Molokai jungle. Everyone yelled a sigh of relief.

"We got lucky folks!" Bella announced joyfully. "It must have been a prototype and malfunctioned. Hopefully there aren't anymore."

"I second that, Agent Walker. Alright teams, time to move in." Rachel advised the teams.

Bella felt the shake of her helicopter as the winds gusted for the final approach and extraction. Her stomach did a flip or two as she watched each of her team rope down to the jungle below. Bella made a last check of her gear and harness then roped down fifty feet to the swaying jungle below. Once on the ground and unharnessed, Bella began her advance. With her carbine rifle raised and ready, her team slowly and doggedly crawled over rocks and dense jungle in the fog-covered darkness of the eerie night, toward the western point of the Yellowrock compound.

Rachel took a deep breath as she too felt the rattle of her chopper coming to fifty feet in a clearing east of the Kalaupapa Peninsula. Adjusting her harness and checking the carbine clips, she launched herself in a controlled manner on the rope below. Landing with a jarring thud, Rachel thought she might have twisted her right ankle. But once again, luck prevailed for the team. She recovered quickly, raised her rifle, and proceeded to follow her team to the eastern entrance point of the Yellowrock compound. All the while their Venom helicopter provided cover.

George cracked his neck and looked over at his team's response to the rough waves off the Molokai coast.

"Good luck, team," he murmured. Despite his reputation as the local jokester, George was the most sentimental of the team. Currently, he was hoping that no more spooky sights came for the team on Halloween

Night. He and Charlie Team were mere miles offshore, cautiously moving in to find the best place to spread out.

As another swell lifted the bow of his fast attack boat, he pondered.

*It's nights like these that make me think I should take that quiet office job up in the Rockies.*

Billy heard the crash of a wave across the bow. He looked over to Keith who seemed to be napping in the darkness of the boat. He and Delta Team proceeded from the north westerly position in the second armada of SEAL crafts. Their journey too had been racked with treacherous, rolling swells and crashing waves as they approached the shore. Their boat captain had done his best trying to stay fixed awaiting orders to advance, but it had been impossible for their team to remain on point with the constant battering of the sea. Hopefully, the same issues plaguing the boat teams would prevent Yellowrock from even thinking of a sea or river escape.

"Echo and everyone, be on guard this round with the cave systems and lava tubes. We don't want a repeat of Waimea Canyon," SAC Harris warned as the teams made their arduous treks and sails inward to pin down and capture Sure-Kill and her cronies.

With a yawn, he looked over to Agent Roberts and Agent Namara as their Viper made its close descent to drop them off on a flat field a few miles south of the Yellowrock Compound. He caught a moment of nostalgia as he watched Natalie adjusting her harness nervously about to plunge out of a perfectly good helicopter. Then he looked over to the geared-up Agent Namara who had seen him smile as Natalie dropped out to the dark jungle below.

"You two were an item once, sir?" Agent Namara yelled over the whir of the helicopter blades and the wind. Susan asked as she set her feet wide to rope out next from the helicopter.

"No. I was too into my career and capturing bad guys, Agent Namara." Director Harris yelled back and shrugged. "We could have been, though. She sailed away on that ship with Algernon Magnum long ago."

# CHAPTER TWENTY-TWO

***Kalaupapa Peninsula***
***Kalaupapa, Hawaii***
***November 1st, 2023***
***05:30 A.M.***

THE FIRST RAYS OF SUNLIGHT SLOWLY BEGAN TO ILLUMINATE BOTH the seas and jungles of Molokai. As blankets of fog covered both the shards of light inched slowly to burn off its damp, cool cover. But while the damp condensation and darkness had proved a nuisance for the teams drenching them and making step a slippery mess, it had concealed their movements to advance and capture Yellowrock.

Four hundred feet outside the cinder block and razor wired walls of the Yellowrock compound, as Bella bent to adjust her combat boot, the first spurts of gunfire rang out in the humid air. She heard the whiz of bullets in front of her and the orange blaze of the rifles alight. Ducking low, she and her team returned fire. Moving down to get a better shot, Bella and Alpha Team ducked behind several fallen logs near a winding river. They waited for the next round. At first there was nothing but stillness and the lapping waters of the river. Then the Yellowrock assailant hit them with another tight round of fire.

Then Bella heard something unnerving and felt the jungle around her moving as if a thunderous earthquake was about to proceed. She looked around worriedly, but Lieutenant Child gave her a broad grin and a wink.

*We are in the middle of a possible earthquake or eruption on Molokai during a gunfight. And this crazy fool winks!*

Then Bella realized the reason for the man's grin. From the left, from the right, and behind their attackers, came the descent of several advanced drones, the most state-of-the-art military equipment ever devised—except for that created by Yellowrock, of course. The drones flew in at breakneck speed and dropped targeted charge bombs on the area in a sweep so fast she didn't see it coming.

The Yellowrock men scrambled to launch several of their own drones, but they were too late. The second wave of drones flew through mere seconds after the first, but this time, they unleashed a very different kind of weapon.

There was a sudden shift in the air. It was like the cessation of one kind of noise and the beginning of chaos. For the low electrical humming of the entire base—all the lights, generators, radio chatter, and all manner of electronic interference—suddenly ceased. And then all the drones, from both sides, began crashing into the earth.

"What the hell—"

"Damn drones—"

More shouts of frustration and confusion burst forth as the Yellowrock men tried to figure out how to defend themselves. They were already busy putting out the fires of the first wave of bombing, and with debris crashing all over the base and their communications cut off, they had nowhere left to turn.

Bella shook her head to scold Lieutenant Child. "You could have told me we had EMPs before the assault, Lieutenant."

"And where would have been the fun in that, Agent Walker?" he replied.

Bella raised her rifle and stormed the gates as the assault teams poured in through the doors.

That had been the final straw to break the last remaining Yellowrock mercenaries. With their camp destroyed and colleagues surrendering, the rest of Yellowrock's mercenaries put their hands up or put their arms behind their heads and went to their knees. Those trying to escape were instantly caught by Echo Team.

The only remaining Yellowrock hold out not found—yet—was Sure-Kill.

# CHAPTER TWENTY-THREE

***Kalaupapa Peninsula***
***Kalaupapa, Hawaii***
***November 1st, 2023***
***8:30 A.M.***

WITH THE COMPOUND IN A BLAZING, SMOKEY MESS, BUT SECURED, Bella sat resting her aching legs. Traversing the jungle in full assault gear and weapons with her team had been the usual slippery, knee-wracking mess it had always been. Looking toward the fire teams trying to quench the blaze most likely set by Yellowrock to destroy evidence, Bella waited as each of the teams arrived with her colleagues. She didn't have to wait long.

"I see Yellowrock will be going out of business," smiled Keith Benton as he came walking through the blasted-open north front gate.

"It seems so, Agent Benton." Bella stood and stretched her aching neck.

"I wouldn't be so sure. These guys always have a team of lawyers to declare bankruptcy to start over." George walked in from the northwestern side of the compound past a smoldering hummer.

"Aren't you the bearer of great news, Agent Dwyer." Rachel lamented as she climbed over a fallen palm.

She, Susan, and Director Harris approached out of the jungle from the south.

"Where's Aunt Natalie?" Bella looked around concerned. She should have been with the Echo Team, who were helping dousing water on the main Yellowrock offices.

"I'd thought you'd have seen me by now, Bella," Natalie called down from a watch tower overlooking all the team's activities. And from what Bella could see, her perch was air conditioned. The power had come back on after only an hour—more than long enough to secure and round up every Yellowrock operator on site. Lieutenant Child hadn't revealed how the one-hour EMP burst had worked or where it had come from, but something told her she was going to have to sign a waiver before the day was done.

Harris chuckled as he looked up to Natalie. "You always find the best locations after a gun battle, Agent Roberts. Did you find our missing assassin?"

"She's floundering and falling that way. If we don't send hovercraft now, she might drown in the quicksand." Natalie pointed to the southeastern jungle and the Molokai Forest Reserve.

"That sounds like an excellent plan. We'll get the SEALs to drop us off in front of her and close in." Harris took a deep sigh, narrowed his eyes and gave everyone a concerned look as he looked on the team. "This is the end game for Codename Sure-Kill. She has nothing to lose and is dangerously desperate. Make sure you don't get sloppy and become a sure kill for her."

"Very funny, sir," said Rachel.

It took the teams ten minutes to be dropped by the hovers into the surrounding thick jungles of Molokai. With a perimeter circle and backup personnel enclosing the deadly assassin, Bella and her team scrambled over rock, log, and stream in pursuit of their target. All teams spread out pushing their advance into the treacherous higher climes of Molokai.

As they climbed, Bella caught Keith as he slipped on wet palms and almost dropped headfirst into a river. Luckily his rifle strap caught a nearby stump and prevented that. A few minutes later, Bella felt the ground give and caught a vine preventing her from falling into another of Hawaii's notorious lava tubes. She heard a snicker from George who caught sight of the event from his vantage point on a nearby ancient tree.

Winding across a twisted and turning ravine, Bella noted the birds had stopped their calls. Bella scanned as she meandered around another bend—still no animal activity or bird calls. She proceeded slowly looking to see her other team members to warn them. She moved slowly, trying not to crack a twig, or rustle the piles of leaves that had fallen from a nearby banyan tree. She scanned up, out, and from left to right, but saw nothing.

Suddenly Bella felt a thud like a large log had dropped on her back, knocking her to the ground. The log had fallen from a nearby rock outcrop as Bella crossed under it. But then Bella realized it wasn't a log but a person twisting to pin her. Her rifle went flying and she saw a pale woman's hand dart out to stop her from reaching for her pistol. In the same instant, Bella caught the smell of sweat on her back and saw another hand—the woman's left hand—trying to stab her with a black, needled cylinder.

There was no time in the moment to think, as Sure-Kill was driving the deadly cylinder and needle closer to Bella's body for the fatal strike. Dropping to her knees, Bella used her weight to throw her would-be assassin from her back, using her weight and momentum against her. Another second and Bella Walker would have been poisoned.

"Why won't you die already?" Hissing like a venomous viper, Sure-Kill slammed her hand in the black jungle ground with a rage. Then as Bella raised her pistol to shoot, Sure-Kill darted into the emerald and yellow bushes of the Molokai jungle.

The rest of the team had already opened fire the moment Bella broke free of the woman's grasp, but somehow, she seemed to slide between the bullets and disappear.

Bella took a nervous breath, listening and watching the forest around her cautiously, and carefully. She knew Sure-Kill was still lingering somewhere in the shadows of the dark jungle waiting to attack again.

# CHAPTER TWENTY-FOUR

Aunt Natalie walked up to help Bella to her feet. "Are you okay?" Bella stood as George reached them and picked up her fallen rifle.

Bella knocked dirt and leaves off her shoulders and back. "I'll be a little sore for the next week. Otherwise, I'm okay. We need to backtrack, as this gorge tells me she can't advance any further without climbing gear."

"I had a feeling you'd say that." George wiped a layer of salted sweat from his brow. Then the team turned and spread out, backtracking their course across the Molokai jungle.

Two hours and several miles of climbing and trudging through the dense brush, Bella saw Keith and the rest of the team giving shrugs and raising their hands, telling everyone they had seen no sign of Sure-Kill. Bella groaned learning that even Aunt Natalie had seen nothing.

*Finding a group of people with all three hundred of our personnel and hovers would be a miraculous task. And here we are trying to find a single assassin who is obviously trained in jungle survival… and warfare.*

Bella took a tired breath and leaned on a nearby grayish black rock, taking the briefest of moments to bend a knee to adjust her rifle strap. Bella narrowed her eyes and furrowed her sweat-soaked brow, studying the walk before her. Thirty feet from her loomed a lurking, monstrous acacia tree. The twisting, grotesque tree held all manner of shadowy cave-like shelters and winding stairs to climb far above the canopy. It was the perfect place in all the dense Molokai forest to conceal or shelter a deadly killer.

Bella heard the whistle and whir of something launching itself out of the emerald bush. Then she caught the glimmer of silver—too late—before she felt a stinging burn to her left upper arm. Ducking behind the rock, she saw her left sleeve had been cut and she had a minor knife gash to upper arm, most likely some form of throwing knife. The split-second thought crossed her mind that she hoped the blade hadn't been laced with poison. Then Bella heard a cracking branch and saw the shuffle of leaves as Sure-Kill poised to launch a second throwing knife to kill her.

Bella ran without hesitating. She bolted like a lioness, tackling her would-be assassin. Sure-Kill in response tried to throw a roundhouse kick to knock Bella astride. Bella countered with a sharp shin strike of her own, toppling Sure-Kill. In the melee, Sure-Kill reached instinctively for a black poison cylinder on her hip. To stop her Bella launched a lateral side kick knocking the lethal assassin off balance. It was a narrow graze as Sure-Kill twisted to avoid the strike and stab Bella with the retrieved autoinjector.

Bella lashed out with her hand to strike the assassin's wrist, in hopes of knocking the injector from her hand. The woman moved her hand out of the way, but that was just what Bella wanted—she pressed forward with a hard, low kick to the woman's ankle, which sent her stumbling backward. Bella decided to scramble back instead of pressing her advantage, using the moment to regroup and grab her gun.

But she very nearly waited too long. Sure-Kill was already leaping forward, the murderous glare in her eyes glinting in the sun.

As she moved in for the final lethal blow to kill Bella, an enraged Tatiana Morozova screamed out, "Die, damn you, once and for all!"

Bella fired off a shot, but it only glanced against the woman's arm. Not enough to stop her momentum.

Bella covered her face with both her arms defensively, hoping Sure-Kill's jab would miss. But knowing in palpable dread that Sure-Kill never missed.

A moment passed. A moment long enough for Bella to realize that something had gone awry. Then she heard a horrific squealing as if someone were wheezing. It was followed by a slurping, fluidic sound of someone drowning. Bella lowered her arms, relieved that she hadn't been stabbed by Tatiana Morozova's poisonous cocktail. But puzzled all the same.

She lifted herself up to see her answer. Sure-Kill had fallen to her knees gasping for air. The woman's face had gone pale and ashen as the vessels in her neck bulged and twisted as writhing snakes. Foam—pink, froth, and copious—oozed from her mouth. Then seizing, Bella realized what had caused the woman's demise.

Bella's gunshot had caused the injector to drop from her hand. As Tatiana Morozova shook and shuddered, Bella caught the glimpse of the black cylinder—the lethal poison injector—stuck in the assassin's right leg.

Sure-Kill, Yellowrock's number one assassin, had accidentally poisoned herself.

George, Susan, Billy, and Keith ran up and stared stunned at the horrific scene of the dying Sure-Kill.

Natalie walked up and over to the dying killer and stooped down as Bella immediately called for a medevac for Tatiana Morozova. Putting her hands together almost in a prayer, Natalie lowered her head and whispered an ominous quote from William Faulkner's 'A Rose for Emily'.

*"The body had apparently once lain in the attitude of an embrace, but now the long sleep that outlasts love, that conquers even the grimace of love, had cuckolded him."*

Keith stooped down beside Natalie and whispered. "What's the long sleep that outlasts love?"

"Mr. Faulkner called it the 'long sleep' in his writings," she shrugged. "But we call it death."

Bella took a deep controlled breath trying to calm her racing heart. "Come in, Medevac Team. This is Agent Walker."

"This is Medevac Team, Agent Walker. How can we assist?" they responded with the whir of chopper blades in the background.

Bella looked grimly at the still seizing, frothing Sure-Kill. She saw her whole team had put their heads down solemnly after gazing at the dying woman. "We need a medevac at our location as soon as possible. It looks like Sure-Kill has made her last kill."

# CHAPTER TWENTY-FIVE

***Molokai Police Department***
***74-88 Ainoa St***
***Kaunakakai, Hawaii***
***November 2nd, 2023***
***09:00 A.M.***

BELLA WATCHED CAREFULLY AS HARRY FINCH WAS BROUGHT BACK into MPD's interrogation room. She studied the man as he used his handcuffed hands to brush back his silken hair with all the arrogance of a royal aristocrat or a king. She watched in irritation as he tapped his fingers triumphantly and with eager purpose waiting for the FBI to enter.

Bella rolled her eyes over to Director Harris and Rachel who both chuckled. Then she smirked back, "Do you want to do the honors, sir? Or would you like me to entertain his offer?"

Director Harris gave Bella a wry smile and shrugged. "No, I think this dog and pony show is all yours. I'd recommend you put on your most tearful, somber game face. Then give him a ten-minute pause." He ushered the FBI team to chairs with actual bowls of hot buttered popcorn. "All of us will sit here patiently eating popcorn and enjoying the show."

Bella rubbed her eyes. It appeared that she had been crying. And considering that she was already worn out from the adventure yesterday, it didn't take much to make her seem disheveled. Then she frowned over to her boss and the team before opening the creaking door of the interrogation room.

As if the Devil himself sat across from her, Harry Finch had the widest of wicked smiles with the most sympathetic of eyes locked on her. "Agent Walker, I'm truly sorry to see you so upset. Any loss—especially a tragic one such as a beloved aunt—can challenge even the best of us in our faith. I mean how can there be a God if he allows such horrors to be committed by the cruelest of our kind?"

Bella wiped back her tears and lowered her head penitently. "Like Aunt Natalie always taught me, God doesn't commit these crimes. People do. We all have a choice—free will—to abide by the Golden Rule: treating others as you would like to be treated. Most people, I think, adhere to it just fine. Following the rule of law. Helping one another. But some choose not to."

"Your Aunt Natalie was a profoundly wise woman. Though, you must agree at times... reckless." Harry cocked his head slightly and raised his right brow. "You are too much like her. Driven to stop criminals, never realizing that such unwavering dedication has an unbearable cost at some point to your heart, your soul... and your life."

The orange glare of a flickering lightbulb gave Harry a menacing, otherworldly, demonic presence. In the moments after his speech on tragedy and his heartless mannerisms, plus the murders and chaos he had committed, Bella could truly believe this man was something like the bringer of Hell on Earth.

Bella raised her head slightly and sighed sadly. "Yes, Agent Roberts truly was the best the FBI had out there, crushing the evil of this cruel world. Her dedication and self-sacrifice will be greatly missed."

"Well enough of the dead." Harry laid his manicured hands flat on the table as if spreading a sheet. "I have plenty to share on all of Yellowrock's operations across the globe—as well as all the subsidiaries, competitors, you name it. I can give you the accountants that cooked the books—tax fraud and evasion, the warehouses of advanced weaponry like rail guns and the UAP's, plus the names of every assassin from here to Papua New Guinea and beyond. But I'll need conditions of immunity from prosecution and witness protection in writing before I deliver."

"And you are sure you can deliver all these things you have promised?" Bella leaned in with desperate, almost pleading eyes.

Harry lifted his cuffed hands up dismissively. Bella could clearly see his ego had no limits. "Of course, I can, Agent Walker. I was the head of Yellowrock, after all. I can give you all you need on the smaller, more discreet international outfits too. But that intelligence will cost a well-paid fee for delivery. But once my demands are met, I'm an open book."

Bella studied a Styrofoam cup of bitter coffee she had brought into the room. She looked down at the half-filled cup, took a deep, tired breath, then sighed. "I need to get another cup of coffee. Would you like one, Mr. Finch?"

Harry raised his left hand and rubbed his chin with a Cheshire cat grin. "I would absolutely love one, Agent Walker."

Bella stood then turned to leave. She paused at the door before going out. "So, you handled all of the operations and orders for Yellowrock?"

Harry leaned back indignantly and scoffed. "Of course, I did. Every memo and every letter I have as backup will prove my worth to the FBI and intelligence communities."

"Well, it sounds like you have an ironclad deal with the FBI." Bella lied as she opened the door and proceeded out to her team. "I'll be right back to start working out the terms of your deal. And bring you a cup of coffee."

Thirty minutes later, the door to the interrogation room opened. Harry, who had been napping on the desk, smiled sleepily. "At last, my hot cup of—"

"I hope you like it black, Mr. Finch." Natalie smiled warmly at the shocked former executive of Yellowrock. "They were out of cream and sugar."

Bella strolled in right behind Natalie with her own knowing, mischievous grin. She produced from under arm a pile of documents recovered from the burning Yellowrock compound. The letters and orders signed by CEO Harry Finch outlining procedures and personnel for multiple murders of high-level government officials and FBI agents. One of the orders found was quite damning. "So, I'm afraid your deal is off the table, Mr. Finch. But if you sing like a bird. I'm sure we can cage you somewhere all these powerful people won't kill you."

"But… but… my family?" Harry had begun to sweat slightly and chatter nervously.

"Do you mean the two parrots and the goldfish? Because that's the only family we've found in the books. Unless…" Bella leaned on the wall and crossed her arms.

Stuttering and stumbling his words, Harry rapidly fired his words. "In the Philippines, Josephine! And my sons Alonzo, Aldridge, Adam, and Adrian. I kept them out of anything with Yellowrock for a reason. These people I work for—"

"Harry Finch, you are quite the dastardly find, aren't you!" Natalie shook her head and laughed heartily with Bella. "You mean the family you abandoned twelve years ago? Yes, they are safe. Your ex-wife is remarried to a kind expat from Hamburg, Germany. Apparently, he treats her like a queen. Your sons went off to Ivy League colleges and are now running honest and successful businesses. I'm guessing the real family you are trying to 'protect' is your recent ex-girlfriend who left you three months ago. If she's forced into witness protection with you, she can't run off anymore."

Realizing his family ruse was up, Harry seemed to regroup for a moment. Rubbing back his slick and polished hair with his cuffed hands, he looked down at the table for a minute then back up to Bella and Natalie. "Those are just copies of documents. They are forgeries at best by some in the business and intelligence communities. To others who would protect what I know at all costs, they will be fabrications by a desperate and overreaching FBI. I ask you; doesn't the FBI have enough scandals to wade through to add one more with murky and lurid questions?"

"You know, Agent Walker, he makes a compelling point, doesn't he?" Natalie grinned as she turned a laptop that Bella had brought in just for the occasion.

Bella walked up and pressed an audio and video file labeled poignantly enough Natalie Roberts Elimination. "But then Agent Roberts, Tatiana Morozova, who realized her fine and loyal Yellowrock CEO had a tendency to backstab her assassin colleagues—literally—made recordings with the help of many, many disgruntled employees. Apparently, while they followed your orders out of fear, it didn't sit well with the Yellowrock rank and file that you killed off one of your own who had retired."

Harry shrugged and put his hands out in a leisurely wave. "Again, I tell you sadly, Agent Roberts—By the way, I'm glad you're back from the dead—"

Aunt Natalie interrupted, throwing her would-be murderer off his game. "It feels great to be among the living. Thank you, Harry. I hope the cuffs aren't too snug."

Harry slapped his hands together, rattling his jailor's chains. "Again, those are just altered copies of recordings that my lawyers will have thrown out of court in minutes. We'll prove once again, you used some kind of AI deepfake software to make all these recordings to frame me. Keep in mind, I have the best business and intelligence communities who will defend me at all costs."

"Well, it's settled then." Bella looked at Aunt Natalie and both women shrugged. Then Bella and Natalie rounded up their files and the laptop to leave.

"Wait! What about my deal? I'm willing to work with you to topple down all of it. All the corporate entities running nefarious operations across the globe. Hell, we can shut down over ninety five percent of the human trafficking and drug running across the world, agents." Harry huffed in vehement protest. "You know what I offer is a great deal."

"It was a great deal, Mr. Harry Finch, former CEO of Yellowrock." Bella glanced back dismissively. "But then you tried to assassinate my aunt. You killed off your top employee—a ruthless killer but still a loyal employee—and your employees hate your guts. We have over one hundred of them in custody and all want to work with the FBI. Each has a pivotal piece and on the ground insight into Yellowrock's day-to-day. The best part, none of them tried to kill my aunt."

"Wait!" Harry pleaded as Bella and Aunt Natalie walked out and slammed the door.

Bella waited five minutes before returning to the room. She had one more thing to say to the depraved man before he spent his final days in federal lockdown. Well, maybe, someone else's words in this instance. A woman who had waited a long time to speak her words. A murdered woman or Ghost-in-the-Machine simulation that compelled Bella to say her thoughts and her feelings from beyond… or not.

"Candace hated your guts, you know." Bella stood in the shadows as Harry kept his head low knowing he had played all his cards.

"Oh, you knew her, Agent Walker?" He lifted his head slowly and raised his furious eyes in contempt of her besting him. "I find it funny that a goody-two-shoes like you ever knew the cold-blooded killer I trained. She knew crossing me wasn't going to end well."

Bella realized that Harry, in his utter disgust, had given Bella an actual confession. She pressed a little further using her recollections to press the man. Bella used one of Candace's last phrases that always drove Harry Finch into a maniacal rage through the years she worked for him.

"You'd be surprised who my friends are sometimes, mister. The sheer hubris of your ego, I tell you, Harry, knows no limits."

"What did you just say to me, you useless clown of a woman?" Harry launched forward trying to attack Bella, but he caught himself on the chain. Bella recoiled from his threatening advance awaiting the words to cage the Finch. "How could you possibly know what she said to me? How did you know English Ivy said those exact words?"

"And when did she say them, Mr. Finch?"

"When… when I killed her."

Harry took an anguished sigh as tears fell from his eyes. The nightly hauntings he would endure from the real ghost of Candace Kincaid for all his days behind bars, was one of the few times Bella could empathize with Harry Finch. Thankfully, Bella's haunting had ended when Victor Shelley turned off the machine.

Wide-eyed, with his teeth bared, he lunged again at Bella as MPD entered and hauled him to jail. Bella heard him scream angrily, "It's impossible! There was no way she was alive to say anything to you, Agent Walker!"

Bella screamed back indignantly letting Harry know she'd put the final nail in his coffin. "You killed Candace Kincaid because she was leaving Yellowrock! You ordered her to kill her husband, then you took care of loose ends yourself! Then being the spineless coward you are, you had Sure-Kill lined up to take the fall for Candace's murder. No wonder Sure-Kill betrayed you too. She dimed you out for the feckless hood that you really are."

"I… I can explain…"

"You've explained enough, Mr. Finch. Enough to dig your own grave."

Bella turned on her heel and left him sobbing in the darkness.

# EPILOGUE

***The North Shore***
***Somewhere Off the Northeastern Coast***
***Oahu, Hawaii***
***November 7th, 2023***
***12:00 P.M.***

BELLA HEARD THE TATTER OF SAILS AS A GALE FORCE WIND BROKE, bringing the smell of brine and warm sea spray across the bow of The Salty Pirate. She lowered her head as the keel cut through a wave, dousing all on board with a mighty splash to everyone's delight. Algernon turned his ship's wheel sharp, trying in earnest to correct course before he was run aground by a marauder in his rear.

The gaining vessel was a carbon fiber and foam thirty-foot sailing ship that cut the turbulent seas like a knife through butter. The lightweight Dacron sails of the blasted scoundrel sounded like the whispers of a wraith while they ran to cut across The Salty Pirate's starboard bow.

Cursing under his breath, Algernon cast away his painter and threw caution to the wind—literally—as he had Aunt Natalie and Justin unfurl his secret weapon, a third sail also made of the lightweight Dacron.

With the adjustment, the vanquished captain of the Pineapple Pride spun out and darted in the opposite direction. She sent out her own curses and slurs of disgust while shaking an angry fist.

All the while the old pirate danced a jig with his crew and sang a shanty in his gravelly parrot voice that went like this:

*The prize was ours, my bloodthirsty crew are a' wailing,*
*Precious treasures we gathered beneath silver mist and starlight,*
*For fast is the prow of The Salty Pirate we be sailing,*
*While we gather the gold that ne'er falls through hands in the sunlight,*
*Our adversary looks forward to emeralds from spoils they seek to plunder,*
*But my green treasures I've buried they will forever dig for in vain,*
*Fools they be chasing trinkets while stumbling in my wake and thunder,*
*Avast, me hearties! Let me go to my treasure house under the main!*

Everyone—Justin, Natalie, Bella, and of course, Algernon the bad crooner himself—slapped their legs and laughed heartily.

The Salty Pirate crew passed a fluorescent buoy signaling with a ringing brass ship's bell. The ringing bell indicated that they had indeed won the first round of the sailing prize. Of course, however, there was still enough daylight blazing for another race between the two ships. And maybe Rachel Gentry's Pineapple Pride and her crew could get a rematch. But for now, it was noon and time for both crews to drop anchor and enjoy a well-earned lunch. Which Bella prayed was in a calmer and quieter lagoon.

Pulling both vessels to within ten miles off the coast, Justin and Algernon set anchors and placed The Salty Pirate in a northerly heading to steady the boat in a headwind from the nearby lagoon. Bella moved with Aunt Natalie, steadying herself as Algernon and Justin adjusted the seating and table out for everyone to sit and eat.

Bella studied the nimble, weathered captain of The Salty Pirate and his attention to meticulous detail even when he cooked. It was just a few lobster rolls, but she noted he put the absolute exact amount of spice and seasoning rub to each lobster tail. He put no more than an inch of butter to sauté the tails after the boil. He and Justin cut the vegetables for their salads at just the right angles and size. And all the while he kept a loving eye on Natalie Roberts between meal prepping. Wrapping up the meal with exquisitely designed rose patterned plates, Algernon made sure the even portions were the exact same for each of his guests.

After eating and laughing a spell over the team's recent exploits, more tales were told. Algernon and Justin recalled and argued over Justin's misadventure being chased by a hog in a remote jungle. Algernon and Aunt Natalie had a tussle over how she had fallen overboard as they crossed the Mid-Atlantic. Then Aunt Natalie laughed and laughed some more as a red-faced Algernon went over the embarrassing details of almost sailing himself and Natalie to the North Pole.

Algernon shrugged sheepishly and got everyone laughing again. "I guess, my dear, that was a serious navigational error."

Hooting and hollering with her sides hurting, Aunt Natalie added, "Do you think so, Captain Magnum? I mean we almost spent winter with Santa Claus!"

Bella, with all the laughs and merriment felt the time was right to ask the next all-important question. "Now, how is it that you met my Aunt Natalie, skipper?" Before he could answer, Bella followed up with another important question. "And Aunt Natalie—what made you want to sail the world with him?"

Algernon looked at Aunt Natalie then back to Bella with a narrowed stare and a raised brow. He looked back to Aunt Natalie who put her hands palms up and shrugged.

"I was voyaging through remote Indonesia headed to Papua New Guinea. Well, I was in the midst of a tempest—a vicious swirl of a storm. Nasty business. Lightning had crashed, blasting my navigation and the winds tattered my sails before I could furl them. And as if that hadn't been bad enough, two massive waterspouts ripped just twenty miles away on both sides of The Salty Pirate, nearly capsizing her. I thought for sure when those came through I'd be a goner. Anyway, with my ship wrecked and sinking, I was cast adrift with no rudder and a wrecked prop. Somehow, I caught a break and managed to celestial navigate by one ripped sail to an unmapped Indonesian island."

"And she was on the beach and swam out to rescue you?" Justin gave his former boss a mischievous half-smile.

"No, I saved her from a vicious tribe of man-eating chimpanzees. You see they had—"

"Algae, you had to use monkeys as the villains? I would have thought it would have been vampire bats housed in a stone god or a giant squid." Aunt Natalie rolled her eyes and shook her head. "Do you see why I went on a few adventures around the world with him? This man has his faults and misadventures—some we will never discuss—but boring is not one of them."

She laughed and launched into her version of the story. "We met while Algernon was on leave near Kuala Lumpur. He was out swimming a few miles in open, shark-infested waters and I was reading over my reports. Before I knew it, I had water spots on my report and this funny lookin' red-haired fellow was pleading with me to pull a crab off his foot." Aunt Natalie gave the salty pirate a smirk as she tapped his leg scolding him. "I should have known something was afoot with him at that moment. It wasn't until months later that he confessed he'd put the crab on his foot because he didn't know how else to strike up a conversation with me."

"Algernon, you actually used the crab pick-up line that Spanky Mura had told you was a guaranteed chick attractant? Wait… now I know why he was always calling you Crab Daddy!" Justin howled with bellowing laughter as Bella and everyone followed suit. Well, everyone but Algernon 'Crab Daddy' Magnum. He might have grumbled a word or two to make a sailor blush.

There was the ringing of a brass bell on the port side of the Salty Pirate. Bella heard Rachel's husband Shane Gentry yell in the worst pirate impression next to her own. "Avast, you scallywags! We will take the prize this time!"

As Bella, Natalie, and Justin raced to pull the anchor and set sail, she looked over grinning to her FBI colleagues-turned-sailors. She saw the panther-quick Billy Makani winding the windlass and waved. Susan gave a hearty wave while pushing back her windblown hair. She almost fell over the side giggling as Keith and George were attempting to unfurl The Pineapple Pride's two sails. She waved as Shane put his hands up, shaking his head at the two veteran agents as Keith nearly fell in. Rachel face palmed watching the melee at the steering and rubbed her temples.

Obviously with a few minutes to spare, Algernon waited for The Pineapple Pride's crew to unfurl and prepare. Bella looked over to her friends then back toward the towering mountains of beautiful Hawaii. There was a certain peace, a feeling of ease as she watched the gentle sway of the coconut palms across the brilliant white sands of the coastline. She took a deep breath and sighed.

Powerful arms gently wrapped around her. She looked up to a nervous, slightly sweating, but grinning Justin Trestle. Then Bella herself glanced nervously, staring intensely around to everyone grinning. Even the entire crew of the Pineapple Pride had stopped their sailing chores in anticipation. Then Bella shook her head and grimaced. The Pineapple Pride's hangup had all been a clever ruse.

Gulping, Bella was afraid to turn around for some reason as Justin released his hug. Taking a panicked breath, Bella turned wide-eyed to see a shaking Justin Trestle go to one knee with the largest jewelry box Bella had ever seen.

"Now, I know we've been on many adventures, Bella Walker. But I've been thinking this might be the greatest one of all. So, I'd like to request—will you do me the honor and become my wife?"

Justin raised the open box with the largest diamond engagement ring she had ever seen. Bella was stunned beyond words. She felt her throat tighten and her tongue become coarse sandpaper. On the verge of hyperventilating and swooning, Bella went to say, "Y—"

*Bloop!*

Bella accidentally dropped the ring over the side.

Two excruciating long hours and four scuba tanks later, the team was about to give up the search for Bella's lost engagement ring. Then on a perch at a depth of twenty feet, Bella spotted a glimmer of hope and raced to the edge of a coral outcrop. There, as if it had always belonged on the straw-like coral fan, was her shiny, gold ring. Pulling the ring gently off the flaming red and orange coral, she watched as Justin swam up and pointed. Bella gulped and went still with fear for only the second time of the day. Swimming to her right, forty feet away was—of all things—a tiger shark.

With narrowed eyes and a scolding, warning glare, Bella mouthed a warning to her daredevil, tiger-shark-riding fiancé, "Don't even think about it mister!"

It was three o'clock in the afternoon with both boats tied up alongside in the still lagoon. Everyone was excited about the big news with Bella and Justin and obvious tears and laughs were in order. After another hour of celebrating with champagne and ice cream, Bella caught a curious sight. Rachel and a grinning Shane made haste to get on The Pineapple Pride with the rest of her crew. Then the brass bell rang on both ships.

Algernon roared as Aunt Natalie bellowed with him, "Ahoy mates! Raise the sails, we steer for the sunset! The prize shall be ours again, scallywags!"

And with those epic words from Algernon and Natalie, Bella nudged into the warmth of her beloved mountain of a man. They set forth on another epic journey out across the vast blue sea. With Justin by her side, Bella Walker indeed sailed off... into the sunset.

# AUTHOR'S NOTE

Dear Reader,

We want to thank you for choosing to read The Last Aloha, the third and final installment in the Bella Walker series. My co-author, Thomas York, and I are overwhelmed with gratitude for your support, your enthusiasm, and your commitment to this cast of characters as it has been nothing short of inspiring. As indie authors, it is no small feat to attract readers to our work. By simply reading our work, you have already given us more than enough support. However, if you could spare a few seconds, we would genuinely appreciate it if you could take a moment out of your day to write a review for this novel. Just a few words or sentences would mean the world to us.

Completing this trilogy has been an adventure in itself. To see it through to the final chapter has been both a joy and a challenge. I hope that as you turned the last pages, you found the conclusion both thrilling and satisfying, bringing a sense of closure to the storyline and characters that we've explored together. While this might be the final installment in this particular saga, I hope the memories created within these pages stay with you. The journey might end here, but there are plenty more exciting adventures that await.

If you are looking for another thrilling adventure with a strong female lead, I invite you to experience the latest book in the Emma Griffin® FBI Mystery series, The Girl and the Secret Passage. In this gripping tale, after the horrific killings of two young people, the murder investigation immediately takes on another twisted turn as the killings are linked to bloody and cryptic passages within books from the college library. With shocking clues leaving the local police bewildered and desperate, they called on the FBI to spearhead the investigation. But the nightmare is far from over. More students fall victim to the bloodthirsty killer, and when the rookie agent in charge of the Campus Killer case is critically injured, the experienced Emma Griffin steps in to bring this demented serial killer to justice.

Thank you once again for embarking on this thrilling journey with us!

Yours,
A.J. Rivers & Thomas York

P.S. If for some reason you didn't like this book or found typos or other errors, please let me know personally. I do my best to read and respond to every email at mailto:aj@riversthrillers.com

P.P.S. If you would like to stay up-to-date with me and my latest releases I invite you to visit my Linktree page at *www.linktr.ee/a.j.rivers* to subscribe to my newsletter and receive a free copy of my book, Edge of the Woods. You can also follow me on my social media accounts for behind-the-scenes glimpses and sneak peeks of my upcoming projects, or even sign up for text notifications. I can't wait to connect with you!

# ALSO BY

## A.J. RIVERS

*Book Two— The Girl on Hallow's Eve**

*Book Three— The Girl and the Christmas Past**

*Book Four— The Girl and the Winter Bones**

*Book Five— The Girl on the Retreat**

**Season Four**

*Book Twenty-Two — The Girl and the Deadly Secrets**

*Book Twenty-Three — The Girl on the Road**

*Book Twenty-Four — The Girl and the Unexpected Gifts*

*Book Twenty-Five — The Girl and the Secret Passage*

**Ava James FBI Mysteries**

*Book One—The Woman at the Masked Gala**

*Book Two—Ava James and the Forgotten Bones**

*Book Three —The Couple Next Door**

*Book Four — The Cabin on Willow Lake**

*Book Five — The Lake House**

*Book Six — The Ghost of Christmas**

*Book Seven — The Rescue**

*Book Eight — Murder in the Moonlight**

*Book Nine — Behind the Mask**

**Dean Steele FBI Mysteries**

*Book One—The Woman in the Woods**

*Book Two—The Last Survivors*

*Book Three — No Escape*

*Book Four — The Garden of Secrets*

# ALSO BY

## A.J. RIVERS & THOMAS YORK

**Bella Walker FBI Mystery Series**

*Book One—The Girl in Paradise**

*Book Two—Murder on the Sea**

*Book Three— The Last Aloha*

**Other Standalone Novels**

*Gone Woman*

** Also available in audio*

Made in the USA
Monee, IL
19 June 2024

60217793R00097